"I DIDN'T STEAL YOUR [   ]
softly.

A spark of something dark and hungry glinted in the amber depths of his eyes as he approached her.

"I didn't set your haystacks on fire." His hand came up, and the tips of his fingers softly caressed the line of her jaw.

"I didn't cut your fences." The heat of his body reached out to envelop her.

"Or tear down your gates." His thumb moved tenderly over her bottom lip, a feather-light touch that sent shivers racing up and down her spine.

Her gaze searched his face. Her limbs trembled and tingled with a warmth that pulsated through her entire body. She stared into his eyes. "How can I believe you?" she asked, her voice raspy with emotion.

Jake's arms slid around her waist. "I don't want your ranch, Clanci." His lips brushed across hers. "I don't want your horse," he whispered against her throat as his arms tightened around her. "I only want you. . . ."

WHAT ARE *LOVESWEPT* ROMANCES?

They are stories of true romance and touching emotion. We believe those two very important ingredients are constants in our highly sensual and very believable stories in the LOVE-SWEPT line. Our goal is to give you, the reader, stories of consistently high quality that may sometimes make you laugh, sometimes make you cry, but are always fresh and creative and contain many delightful surprises within their pages.

Most romance fans read an enormous number of books. Those they truly love, they keep. Others may be traded with friends and soon forgotten. We hope that each LOVESWEPT romance will be a treasure—a "keeper." We will always try to publish

LOVE STORIES YOU'LL NEVER FORGET
BY AUTHORS YOU'LL ALWAYS REMEMBER

The Editors

Loveswept ®910

THIEF OF MIDNIGHT

CHERYLN BIGGS

BANTAM BOOKS

NEW YORK · TORONTO · LONDON · SYDNEY · AUCKLAND

THIEF OF MIDNIGHT

A Bantam Book / November 1998

ISBN 0-553-44641-X

Published simultaneously in the United States and Canada

*Bantam Books are published by Bantam Books, a division of Bantam Dou-
bleday Dell Publishing Group, Inc. Its trademark, consisting of the words
"Bantam Books" and the portrayal of a rooster, is Registered in U.S.
Patent and Trademark Office and in other countries. Marca Registrada.
Bantam Books, 1540 Broadway, New York, New York 10036.*

PRINTED IN THE UNITED STATES OF AMERICA

OPM   10 9 8 7 6 5 4 3 2 1

ONE

Clanci James knew she should have her head examined for what she was about to do, but what choice did she have? Running a hand nervously through her long hair, she opened the door to Sam's Bar & Grill and paused in the doorway to peer inside. The room was dimly lit and smoke-filled.

She spotted Jake Walker almost immediately. He was standing across the room beside one of the pool tables.

Clanci closed her eyes for a brief second and took a deep breath, summoning her courage.

Her task would have been a heck of a lot easier if he'd been born ugly. Unfortunately for her, he hadn't been. In fact, ugly was about as far away from Jake Walker as New York was from Texas.

Her gaze moved over him appreciatively, even as she reminded herself that he was the last man on the face of the earth she would ever consider getting involved with.

His jeans hugged long, lean legs that seemed made to drape over a saddle, while the cut of his white shirt accentuated every well-honed muscle of his chest and broad shoulders. And beneath the black Stetson that rode low on his forehead and obscured a good portion of his thick, curly black hair was a pair of eyes she already knew were a richer brown than any whiskey on the bartender's shelf.

Clanci shook the frivolous thoughts away. She wasn't there to admire Jake Walker's looks.

Before she could decide on her next move, a woman in a scandalously low-cut western blouse walked up to Jake. She pressed herself against him like a fly to flypaper, one hand moving to rest possessively on his shoulder, the other sliding caressingly up and down his arm.

Clanci watched the woman paw Jake and felt a spurt of annoyance that she instantly shrugged off. Actually, she told herself, the woman just might be doing her a favor. If she managed to keep Jake at the bar, Clanci wouldn't have to do anything after all, and that was just fine with her.

She walked across the room and settled on a bar stool, only a few feet from where Jake and Miss Octopus were draped over each other.

The bartender acknowledged Clanci with a nod. A few minutes later he set the cherry cola she'd ordered down on the bar in front of her, folded his arms, and settled in for a chat. She didn't miss the look of curiosity in his eyes, or the curve of a smile beneath his thick, drooping blond mustache. "Don't see you in here too often anymore, Clanci. What's the occasion tonight?"

She smiled. "Oh, I don't know, Ben. Just felt like getting out for a while, that's all. I didn't realize I'd be watching the R-rated maneuvers of our newest neighbor, though."

"Walker?" Ben laughed, glancing toward Jake and the voluptuous blonde. "Yeah, the women around here sure do like him, that's a fact."

"Not all of them," Clanci said with a sneer, then felt as if the word *liar* had suddenly lit up like a neon sign over her head. Even though she was loath to admit it, she found Jake Walker handsome. But she *did not* "like" him!

Ben's cocktail waitress brought an order to the bar, and he turned away to take care of it.

Clanci sipped on her soda and tried to drown out the background sounds in order to eavesdrop on what Jake and his friends were saying. She watched them in the mirror that covered the back wall of the bar.

"Want to rack up another game, Jake?" the man next to him asked.

"Not tonight, Mr. Harrison. I've got to drive up to Denver tomorrow for a few days, and since I'm planning on leaving at dawn, I figured I'd call it an early night."

Clanci stiffened as alarm swept through her. Early night? He couldn't call it an early night.

That's exactly what she didn't want him to do! What she couldn't let him do. Her mind raced in pursuit of an answer. She tried to sneak a glance at him out of the corner of her eye while praying the blonde still draped across his arm would do or say something to change his plans.

"Oh, Jake, honey," the woman said, "I was hoping you'd stick around a little while longer. I mean, since Timmy only likes to play pool"—she smiled coyly and winked at the other man—"I was hoping you'd dance with me."

Clanci was too annoyed with the woman's clinging-vine type of flirtation to remember she should have felt relief that Miss Octopus was trying to detain Jake.

Jake laughed, and Clanci was surprised to find herself admiring the deep, rich sound that rumbled from his throat. She'd never heard him laugh before.

"Mrs. Harrison, I'm sure there are any number of cowboys in here tonight who would be more than happy to dance with you while your husband plays pool."

"Oh, poo," the woman said, feigning a pout and batting a thick set of false eyelashes at him. "Maybe so, but I had my little ol' heart set on you, didn't I, Timmy?"

Jake smiled. "Sorry. Maybe another time."

In spite of herself, Clanci felt a spurt of relief. What in tarnation was the matter with her anyway? Had she gone completely loco? She *wanted* the woman to detain Jake. Then Clanci wouldn't have to do anything to prevent him from returning home too early and ruining everything.

Jake shook Tim Harrison's hand and said good night.

Clanci muttered a string of curses beneath her breath. So much for the last threads of her hope. Jake was preparing to leave the bar, and she couldn't let that happen. At least not yet. Whirling around on her bar stool, she stared at him and frantically tried to decide what to do as he talked to another man. She could start an argument.

Her fingers drummed nervously on her denim-covered thigh.

Maybe she should accuse him of cutting the wires on the fence that divided their properties; or call him a louse for setting the haystack in the Lazy J's west pasture on fire. Even better, she could damn him for destroying the easement road gate that led to the river.

Except she didn't have any real proof that he'd done any of those things.

Her mind felt as if it was floundering in a sea of indecision. Even if she did try to start an argument with Jake, she knew it wouldn't delay him enough. He'd just growl down her throat and walk off the way he had the two other times her anger had gotten the better of her and she'd confronted him. But she had to do something. And she had to do it now!

She cursed under her breath at remembering how her grandfather had told her to "use her womanly wiles," and realized she was going to try doing just that . . . if she could figure out what her womanly wiles were.

Sliding off of the bar stool, she hurried toward Jake as he turned from the couple he'd been talking to and started for the door.

If he preferred voluptuous, purring bleached blondes who draped themselves over him in public, then she was in trouble. But at least she had to try to keep him from leaving.

Clanci stepped into his path and smiled up at him. "Hi there, Jake."

His gaze raked over her as his dark brows slanted into a frown.

Clanci saw the surprise in his eyes. A natural reaction, since he'd asked her out numerous times and she'd always coldly turned him down. "Care to buy me a drink?" She held up her almost empty glass.

Suspicion gleamed in his eyes and cast a shadow over his rough-hewn features. But she also saw interest in the amber depths of his eyes.

"Sorry, Clanci." He shook his head. "But I was just leaving."

Disappointment that he hadn't jumped at her offer overwhelmed her. Trying to rationalize the unexpected feeling, she told herself the only reason she cared that he'd turned her down was because he was making the task of keeping him there more difficult.

She decided to try again and attempted to look coy, something she had never attempted before. "Oh, that's too bad. I was hoping we could talk awhile, maybe get to know each other a little better."

He didn't respond for several agonizingly long seconds, and Clanci had started to wonder if she'd made a fool out of herself.

"Yeah?" he finally said. An array of featherlike laugh lines crinkled around his eyes as he grinned down at her. "Kind of a real change of heart for you where I'm concerned, isn't it? You usually try to avoid me." One brow arched slightly. "Or roll over me like a steamroller."

She shrugged and cocked one hip sassily, resting her hand on it. "Well, I've been thinking about that and decided maybe I haven't exactly treated you fairly since you moved here. I mean . . ." She swallowed hard. This whole thing was sticking in her craw like a pork chop going down her throat sideways. Admitting she was wrong was something she never did. Ever. And admitting it to Jake Walker made it all the worse. But, she quickly decided, since she was faking this whole thing, she wasn't really admitting to anything, wrong or right. That made her feel better. Clanci smiled. "Maybe I've been wrong about you, Jake. How about it? Want to prove it to me?"

His mercurial eyes bore into hers, then narrowed slightly as he weighed her words. He didn't know what kind of game she was playing; he couldn't deny, however, that she'd piqued his interest. But then, he'd been interested in Clanci James since the very first moment he'd seen her. That had been nine months earlier, and given the fact that she'd turned him down flat every time he'd asked her out, he'd about given up on her returning his interest. "What are you really up to, Clanci?"

Her stomach clenched into a knot as apprehension flickered through her. "Nothing," she said quickly. For some reason she didn't understand, she found looking him directly in the eye and lying at the same time nearly impossible, so she glanced toward the bar. "I just figured that, well, since we're neighbors, maybe we should at least try to get along."

"Really?"

The skepticism that laced his voice was thick enough to slice with a knife. Clanci bristled but managed a tremulous smile. "Yes, but, if you don't agree . . ."

"I'd really like that, Clanci," he said, "but your timing's rotten. I've got an early morning tomorrow, and a long trip ahead of me that I can't postpone. How about giving me a rain check?"

She stiffened. Suspicion still gleamed in his eyes, but she couldn't let that stop her. "Forget it," she said, and shrugged offhandedly. "I thought maybe we could be friends, but if you're too busy even to try talking, I guess we can just go on thoroughly disliking each other." Clanci spun around and walked back to the bar. If this bluff didn't work, her grandfather would kill her . . . if he ever got out of jail after tonight.

Jake shook his head, wondering at his own sanity, and even though some little voice way in the back of his mind yelled that he'd be better off throwing himself into a cactus patch, he followed her. "Ben," he called to the bartender, "bring Clanci another of whatever she's drinking, and I'll have another beer." He leaned lazily against the bar as his gaze moved over her slowly, a blatant assessment that caused her blood to boil and her cheeks to sting.

"I've lived in Coyote Bend for about nine months now, Clanci, and asked you out, what? Six . . . seven times at least? And you've turned me down flat every time." He took a sip of his drink as he watched her and wondered, not for the first time, what there was about Clanci James that intrigued him. She was an attractive woman, there was no denying that. Dark brown hair, touched by a shimmering veil of red, fell about her shoulders in lush waves; she had a pair of the bluest eyes he'd ever seen; and at about five feet eight inches, her body was lithe, well curved, and, he judged, just about the right height and shape to fit nicely against his own.

The thought, not the first such one he'd had about Clanci James, sent a wave of heat speeding through him that caused his body to begin to harden and the inseam of his Levi's to tighten. He shifted position on the stool he'd dropped one hip onto and, leaning an elbow on the bar, cleared his throat. "So tell me, Clanci, just what did I do to deserve this second chance you're offering?"

"Oh, I . . . uh, just thought . . ." She waved

her hand nonchalantly, half-afraid her heart was going to fly out of her chest, it was beating so fast. But whether her nervousness was over carrying out her scheme, or a reaction to the way he'd been looking at her, she wasn't sure. "I, um, don't know really. I just thought, ah, it might be easier to be friends than not, that's all. I mean, after all, everyone deserves a second chance, even you." She could have bit her tongue off for that last comment, but it was too late.

His brows rose slightly and a muscle twitched along the hard line of his jaw. "Well, that's certainly nice of you, Clanci," he drawled. "But maybe it's more that there's no one else in here tonight who interests you at the moment, huh? So you thought you'd talk to me for a while and confirm that I am as big a creep as you think I am."

His brash words surprised Clanci. She stood, more uncertain than ever about what she was supposed to be doing.

The deep chuckle that rippled past his lips softened the words, but she saw something flash briefly into his eyes that made her wonder if he wasn't much more serious than he'd intended to convey. "Sit down, Clanci."

She hesitantly resumed her seat. "I never said you were a creep, Jake."

"That's true. I think the word you used was *jerk*." A smile tipped the corners of his mouth as his gaze remained riveted on hers, as if analyzing her.

She felt the sting of a blush attack her cheeks and silently cursed him to a slow, agonizing death. She was trying to be nice to him, and in return he was being purposely infuriating. "You made me mad."

Jake nodded. He was baiting her, goading her, and he didn't know why. He just knew he was thoroughly enjoying their exchange and didn't want it to end. "Most women don't get mad when a man asks them for a date, Clanci."

She looked into his eyes and for a moment found herself incapable of looking away. When she was finally able to avert her gaze, her pulse was racing, a gnawing ache had coiled deep in the pit of her being, and she swore that her grandfather was going to owe her big time. Spending the entire evening in the company of Jake Walker was not something she'd ever have done voluntarily.

"You want me to prove you right," Jake said. "That I am a jerk."

"Or wrong," she said coyly, hating herself for acting like the flirtatious, game-playing kind of female she despised.

The urge to touch her was suddenly almost overwhelming. "Dance with me," Jake said a moment later when a slow song echoed from the jukebox. He slid off the stool and held out a hand toward her.

Clanci felt a flash of alarm. Dance? That meant body contact . . . arms around each other . . . her breasts touching his chest . . . her hips . . . Her cheeks smoldered as images that matched her thoughts flashed through her mind. She knew all too well that even if a woman disliked a man, she could be physically attracted to him—unfortunately.

His eyes seemed to sparkle, as though sensing her uneasiness and daring her to refuse him.

She did thoroughly dislike Jake Walker. He was a rat. But she couldn't deny that she found him attractive, or that she'd caught herself wondering more than once in the past what it would feel like to be kissed by him.

A tingling sensation sped up her arm as he reached down and took her hand in his.

Clanci's gaze flew up to meet his.

No. She didn't want to dance with him, to get that close to him. She pulled her hand free of his. "I'm . . . I'm really not a very good dancer, Jake. In fact, I'm actually quite horrible at it."

"Let me be the judge of that."

She shook her head. "No, really, I'll just step on your toes."

"So? I'll bet you don't weigh enough to dent the leather."

Before she could stammer out another excuse, he wrapped a strong, warm hand around her arm and gently pulled her to her feet.

"Jake, no, really. You'll be sorry. Believe me. I . . ."

"I doubt that," he said, his husky whisper holding just a trace of quiet laughter. He drew her to him easily and, splaying a hand against the small of her back, pressed her tightly to his length.

Every cell in her body suddenly bolted to attention.

He whirled her onto the dance floor.

Clanci stole a glance at him, forced to look up as the top of her head barely reached the crest of his shoulder.

"I always knew it would feel good to hold you."

Clanci bit down on her bottom lip. Her ex-husband had said something very similar to her on their wedding night. Two years later she'd found herself wondering how many other women he'd used the line on.

She closed her eyes and tried to ignore the pulsing knot that had formed in the pit of her stomach the moment he'd pulled her into his arms, and the warm shivers that the feel of his body pressed to hers was causing to race through her body.

Jake Walker and Alex Tremaine were two of a kind; too handsome, too suave, and too charming. Unfortunately for her she'd found out too late that Alex was also a died-in-the-wool ladies' man. The moment she'd met Jake she had felt no doubt that he was a Lothario, too, which was why she'd always turned him down when he asked her out. The fact that he'd dated at least four or five other local women since moving to Coyote Bend had just proved to her that she'd been right.

"Relax, Clanci," Jake crooned softly into her ear. "I don't bite."

She swallowed hard and tried to ignore the acceleration of every facet of her body. Her heart had begun pounding like an automatic snare drum gone out of control, her pulse was throbbing like mad, and her skin felt as if it were on fire.

It's only nerves, she tried to tell herself. She didn't like Jake Walker. She didn't like him touching her, whispering to her, making her feel things she didn't want to feel. At least not because of him.

She gritted her teeth together and prayed that her grandfather was succeeding with his part of their plan, because if she was going through with this torment for nothing, she would kill somebody.

The music swirled around them as they moved slowly across the nearly empty dance floor. She hadn't been lying when she'd said she wasn't a good dancer, yet she was finding it surprisingly easy—and comfortable—to match her steps to his.

A large and very noisy group of locals entered the bar and confiscated a table in the corner. Jake whirled Clanci around, and she glanced toward the new arrivals as one yelled for the bartender in a voice she was all too afraid she recognized. She was instantly sorry she hadn't buried her face in Jake's chest instead.

"Hey, Clanci," the same man who'd beckoned the bartender called out, spotting her and waving.

The rhinestones on his shirt and hatband caught the overhead light and danced in glistening brilliance.

A groan nearly escaped Clanci's throat as she half smiled, half grimaced at Alex. This evening was quickly turning out to be the worst of her life.

TWO

Her divorce from Alex had been anything but amicable, at least as far as Clanci was concerned, and if she never talked to the man again, it would be too soon. Most people reach the point of loathing each other by the time the judge bangs his gavel down and gives them their freedom from each other. They want nothing more than to go their own way and have as little as possible to do with their ex-spouse.

That was how Clanci felt. To her dismay, however, Alex did not feel the same way. Almost immediately after their divorce became final, he decided he wanted to be her friend again, maybe even her occasional lover. After all, he'd said, they'd always enjoyed each other in bed.

She'd realized then what had actually gone wrong with their marriage: Alex was the type of man who always wanted what he didn't have, which explained all his extramarital affairs. When he didn't "have" Clanci anymore, he wanted her.

She smiled and waved a hand at him, praying that would be the end of it and he'd turn his attention back to the woman sitting beside him.

"Come on over and join us when you're done dancing," Alex called out.

The woman beside him shot Clanci an icy look.

"More like when hell freezes over," Clanci muttered.

"That bad, huh?" Jake said, and leaned back to look down at her.

She gritted her teeth as humiliation swept through every cell of her body. She hadn't meant to speak aloud. "Sorry."

"We all have our regrets," Jake said, and pulled her close again.

Clanci closed her eyes. Alex was indeed a regret, but she'd had others, and before her life was over, she had no doubt there would be more. Her present one was being in the arms of Jake Walker. She figured his regret was not having found a way to get his hands on the ranch she and her grandfather called home.

"Hey, Clanci, got a couple of chairs over here for you and your friend," Alex called out.

"Doesn't give up, does he?" Jake murmured against her ear.

"Jerks never do," she mumbled, then instantly stiffened, remembering that she'd called Jake a jerk. She looked up at him, their eyes met, and for the briefest of seconds she had the strangest feeling that her life had changed. "Sorry. I didn't mean . . ."

Amusement glimmered in his eyes.

Pulling her gaze from his, Clanci told herself she was being ridiculous. She needed to ignore Alex, and relax and concentrate on pretending she was enjoying being with Jake. He had to believe she wanted to be with him, that she *wanted* him. At least long enough for her grandfather to get home safely. She listened to the music, letting it fill her, and slid her arm up over Jake's shoulder. Pressing closer to him, she moved with him easily, as if the two of them standing together in this netherworld of soft music and dim light, arms wrapped around each other, was the most natural thing in the world. "I made a mistake about you," she said softly after a few minutes.

The side of his chin pressed lightly against her temple. "So I'm not a jerk?"

Clanci could feel the warmth of his breath on her cheek, the heat of his hand on her back, the rise and fall of his chest as he breathed. She knew if she laid her cheek against his chest, she would feel rock-hard muscle, and hear the steady thump of his heartbeat. "Hardly."

The music stopped and Jake leaned down to press his lips to the curve of her neck. "I'm glad you changed your mind about me, Clanci James," he said, his deep drawl washing over her like a wall of flame, "and I'd say you dance just fine."

"Hey, Jake, you still going up to Dallas tomorrow?" someone called out.

He straightened at the interruption and looked around the room but didn't release his hold on Clanci. Spotting one of his wranglers at the bar, he smiled. "Yeah, I'm leaving at dawn, Kyle."

"Well, try not to forget to pick up that part for the dozer I need, huh?"

Jake nodded and turned back to look at Clanci. "That reminds me; before we decided to become friends, I'd intended to call it an early night."

Clanci glanced at the big clock on the wall over the bar and nearly sagged in despair. Her grandfather hadn't had enough time yet. She couldn't let Jake leave the bar. Smiling teasingly, she slid her other hand slowly up and over his chest. She was playing with fire, one whose flames were much hotter and much more dangerous than any she'd ever touched.

Her heart hammered against her ribs as excitement coursed through her veins.

Some inner, basic instinct warned her against continuing the charade. Things were getting out of control, turning on her. The urge to run, to put as much distance between herself and Jake Walker was almost overwhelming . . . as was the yearning to stay within the circle of his arms.

He was trying to ruin her grandfather, she reminded herself. He was trying to destroy everything Harlen and Clanci loved. Jake wanted to take their home away from them, the ranch that had been in the James family for over a hundred years, and change the valley into some kind of mega-resort for the rich and famous. She didn't like him, didn't like what he stood for, yet she couldn't ignore the physical feelings that had begun stirring in her.

She looked up and into his eyes. It was the last thing in the world she should have done, and the thought that accompanied the act was just about the last one she wanted to admit to herself. But she couldn't deny it. Being with Jake Walker was not proving to be at all as unpleasant as she had expected. In fact, it wasn't proving to be unpleasant at all.

The moment the thought registered in her mind she tried to push it aside, not wanting to give it any credence. Jake was exactly the wrong kind of man for her. Hollywood handsome, Lothario charming, and all too very sure of himself.

He was just like Alex.

No, she argued. At least Alex had dallied only with single women, as far as she knew. If the rumors she'd heard about Jake in that respect were true, he was actually worse than Alex.

She forced herself to smile at him. Stalling for time, she looked up and studied his face unhurriedly, letting her gaze move slowly from feature to feature, until finally meeting his eyes. Interest gleamed there. She ran her tongue teasingly over her bottom lip. "But do you still want to call it an early night, Jake?"

Thirty minutes and several slow dances later

Clanci knew she'd taken her inexperienced womanly wiles way too far.

"Holding you feels so right, Clanci," Jake whispered. He swayed to the music as his hands roamed her back and his lips moved along the curve of her cheek.

She pulled away, denying that the hot shivers racing up her spine had anything to do with him and everything to do with the heat in the room and the dryness in her throat. "You know what, Jake? I'm thirsty," she said. "Let's get a drink." She waved a hand in front of her face. "Phew, it's really warm in here, don't you think?" Plucking at the front of her blouse, she walked to the bar and picked up her soda.

Jake moved up behind her and slipped his arms around her waist. "Tell me what you want from me, Clanci," he said softly, his lips moving against the curls of her hair, a sensual drawl to his deep voice.

Her breath caught in her throat as the heat of his body pressed to the back of hers infused her with fire. She felt her composure waver, and when she opened her mouth to say something, nothing came out.

She had to stop this—now, before it went too far. Turning in Jake's arms, she smiled up at him. "I want the world, Jake."

His eyes seemed to search her face, reach into her thoughts, and touch her soul. "From me?" he asked huskily.

His seriousness momentarily set her off guard,

but she quickly recouped, reminding herself that like Alex, Jake was a pro at flirting and sweeping women off their feet with his charm and good looks. "Maybe," she quipped, brushing an imaginary lock of hair from her face and laughing nervously.

He slid a hip onto the bar stool next to her, then leaned forward, closing the distance between them.

The touch of his lips upon hers was merely a whisper of contact, like the slightest wind ruffling through the willow trees of the valley, but it was enough to send a shock wave of sensations ripping through Clanci's body.

When he pulled away, she shivered and looked at him in despair, the wild beat of her heart thumping in her ears. She was not supposed to have felt anything!

He was more stunningly virile than she'd realized. More dangerous.

Jake pulled her into his arms. "So, what part of the world do you want first?"

Clanci slipped a finger into the pocket of her jeans. The tip of her finger touched the little packet of "quieting down" potion her grandfather had given her—just in case. She drew it out, holding it hidden in one hand. "Oh, that's a tough question," she hedged, smiling and trying to make light of the conversation.

She pulled the little packet's tab open and, reaching for her own drink, dumped the powder into Jake's beer as her hand passed over his glass.

Being encircled by his arms was playing havoc

with her resolve. She pulled away from him. "Finish your drink, Jake," she said, trying not to acknowledge the sense of guilt that was trying to settle itself upon her shoulders.

He took a long swallow of his beer, then set the glass back onto the bar. "I don't know what happened to change your mind about me, Clanci, but I'm glad you did." He rubbed at his eyes and picked up the glass again.

Clanci glanced quickly at the packet in her hand. She nearly screamed. It was empty! She'd meant to give him only half of it, the way her grandfather had instructed. But in her haste to do it and not be seen, she'd accidentally dumped the whole packet into his drink. Her gaze jumped to his glass. He'd finished it. The entire drink was gone.

She looked back at him, staring into his eyes. "Jake, are you okay?"

He closed his eyes and rubbed at them again. "I don't . . ." He shook his head violently. Once. Twice. Black curls tumbled onto his forehead.

"Jake?"

He squeezed his eyelids shut.

"Jake?" Lord, what if she'd killed him? "Jake, are you all right?" She grabbed at his shoulder and shook it. "Jake, answer me."

The elbow he'd had resting on the bar slipped off, and he fell forward, then caught himself.

Fear settled like a lump in Clanci's throat.

Jake suddenly jumped off of the bar stool, smiled, and swept Clanci into his arms. "I feel wonderful," he declared loudly. "Come on, let's dance, sweetheart." Before she could protest, he whirled her onto the floor, stumbling several times over his own feet.

"Jake, stop, I . . ." She clung to him, afraid if she let go he'd fall to the floor.

"Home," he said, suddenly stopping in the middle of a dizzying whirl.

She opened her mouth to respond, and he waltzed them out the open doorway and into the parking lot.

"Jake, stop."

He staggered against her, and Clanci fought to help him regain his balance without falling. Rather than quiet him down, her grandfather's potion had made him act drunk.

"Home," he said again, throwing an arm up in the air as if he were a general leading a charge.

"Yeah, right, home," Clanci grumbled. "That's exactly where you belong."

"And you," he mumbled. "I want . . . want . . ." He shook his head, grabbed her to him, and captured her lips with his.

The assault of his mouth on hers caused an instant surge of passion to erupt from deep within Clanci, while his hands, holding her at the waist, crushing her into him, were like branding irons burning right through her blouse and into her flesh, searing her with his mark.

She struggled away from him, afraid of the feelings his kiss ignited in her. "Stop," she said with a gasp. "Please."

He leaned against a car and looked at her with eyes red beyond bloodshot. "Come home with me, Clan . . . ci."

She stared at him, laboring for her own breath, her own sanity. What she was feeling was crazy. She should have been repulsed by his kiss. Instead she was fighting off the aftermath of a sweep of desire like nothing she'd ever felt.

Clanci inhaled deeply, released the breath slowly, and ordered herself to calm down, to remember who this man was, why she was with him, and why she so thoroughly disliked him. She turned back to glare at him, yet even as she did she knew she was really furious with herself.

There was no way in blazes she was going to get involved with Jake Walker, unless it was to take him to court and ruin him. And there was definitely no way she was going home with him.

She sighed. But there was no way she could let him drive in the condition he was in either. And he was in that condition because of her.

Clanci glanced across the parking lot. It was a warm night. If she could get him to his truck, maybe he'd pass out, then he could sleep there until morning. If she was lucky, he'd wake up and not remember a thing.

"Come on, Jake." She wrapped an arm around his waist, draped one of his over her shoulders, and prayed her knees wouldn't buckle under his weight.

"Good," he mumbled, and caught her cheek with a kiss. "Lez go home."

She steered him in the direction of a black pickup, which was parked a few yards away. There was only one black pickup truck in Coyote Bend with a cartoon picture of Foghorn Leghorn painted on its tailgate.

Clanci glanced at the rooster caricature as they rounded the truck and wondered why a grown man would have a cartoon on his vehicle. At the driver's door she reached for the handle.

A head covered with white feathers and topped with a flopping red crown suddenly popped up at her from inside the truck's cab. Beady red eyes stared at her.

Clanci screamed, snatched her hand away from the door, and jumped back.

Jake staggered wildly, throwing out his arms. "Whuh?"

She grabbed him just before he lost his balance.

The rooster thrust its chest out, flapped its wings, and crowed loudly, the sound screeching through the open window and echoing on the night air.

"Shud up, Henry," Jake said, and swatted a hand at the big rooster. "Go on."

The bird squawked indignantly and pranced across the seat.

Jake looked back at Clanci. "Tha's King Henry."

Terrified and wide-eyed, she stared at the

rooster. This wasn't happening, she told herself. It wasn't.

She could handle snakes, lizards, spiders, and wild animals. She had grown up on a ranch. She had been bitten, stung, clawed, and slashed. But nothing had ever vanquished the terror instilled in her when she was six and her grandfather's prize rooster had come after her, beak pecking and claws flailing.

King Henry settled down on the passenger seat.

Clanci reached hesitantly for the handle again and swung the door open.

Jake drew her into his arms. "Love you," he slurred.

"Of course you do," she said. "Me and every other woman for several hundred miles around." She saw his head start to lower toward her, and though for one brief millisecond she considered letting him kiss her again, she turned her face to avoid his kiss and pushed against his chest to get him into the truck.

"No, jus' you," he muttered.

She half shoved and half helped him climb into the truck. "There, now sleep it off."

He twisted around and, grabbing her by the wrist before she could shut the door, pulled her into the truck. "Not without you."

THREE

Why had she thought she could do this?

Why had she let her grandfather talk her into even trying? If they didn't both end up in jail, they'd be lucky.

Clanci stared at Jake.

He smiled back crookedly, his hold on her wrist like a vise grip.

The night air had obviously revived him somewhat.

"Get in sha truck, Clan . . . zeee," Jake said.

She shook her head. "No, I . . ." What? Had to go home? She couldn't do that. She had to keep him from going home. It was still too early. But what was she going to do?

Before she could decide, he pulled her toward him, lifting her right off of the ground.

She had about two seconds to resist, which she did, to no avail. Then his lips were on hers again, his arms holding her pressed tightly to him, drawing her onto his lap.

The sexual magnetism that was Jake Walker suddenly enveloped her, overwhelming her every thought and striking a match to the passions that had lain dormant in her for so long. Resistance vanished from her mind. Time became meaningless. Night and day, dark and light melded, swirling around her, through her mind in a kaleidoscope of brilliant colors and impenetrable darkness. His kiss teased and tempted, drew her toward a chasm of emotion that reason warned was an abyss from which there was no return, a place she had no business being. Self-denial and common sense threatened to spin out of control as an ache of desire invaded her body and instilled in her a hunger to know Jake Walker in a way she had known no other man.

Desires, hungers, and yearnings long staved off swept through her. A shiver rippled over her body from head to foot, leaving even the thought of rejection a thing of the past, and vanquishing logic from reality as if it had never existed.

Insidious flashes of longing danced through her head, daring her to give in to them, to him, to the wild, seductive feelings he was arousing in her.

His mouth caressed hers, tender one moment, savage and demanding the next. His tongue was a lethal dart of flame that burned her flesh wherever it touched, stoked her hungers, and made her want things that, deep down, Clanci still knew she shouldn't want. Not from Jake Walker. But she couldn't help herself.

The warnings screaming through the back of her mind went unheeded as his lips played delicious, mind-searing havoc with hers, ravaging her senses, leaving her helpless in the circle of his arms.

"*Squawk!*"

A huge wing suddenly smacked her head.

Clanci jumped back and twisted away from Jake. Her heart hammered madly in a combination of mindless desire and sudden fear. Gasping for breath, she stared at the rooster, her age-old fear stuck like a rock in the middle of her throat.

Jake turned and pushed the bird away with his hand. "Move over, Henry. Get in the back."

The bird squawked again, but stayed on the front seat.

Jake looked back at Clanci, then grabbed his head, groaned, and swayed on the seat. "Oh, damn." He rubbed at his eyes and shook his head.

"Jake?" Remembering that she'd overdosed him with Grandpa's "quieting potion," Clanci's fear for him immediately overrode her fear of the rooster. "Are you all right?"

Oh Lord, she thought, gripping his shoulder, he had to be all right. What would she do if he wasn't?

He moaned and laid his head on the steering wheel.

"Jake?" She shook him.

The rooster squawked and pranced about on the seat, flapping his wings.

Clanci jumped back as he neared.

Jake's shoulders slumped forward.

Clanci glanced warily at the bird, then reached into the truck and pressed a finger to Jake's neck, feeling for his pulse. It was strong. She felt like fainting with relief. At least she hadn't killed him. But what if the sheriff came by and saw him? Climbing into the cab of his truck, she pushed and shoved him from behind the steering wheel.

King Henry eyed her haughtily, and she did her best to ignore him, though being so near the huge bird definitely unnerved her. Her hands were shaking, her palms were sweaty, and her stomach had a knot in it the size of Rhode Island.

She inhaled deeply and called on every ounce of courage she possessed. Walker Acres was adjacent to the Jameses' Lazy J ranch. She would just drive Jake home, park his truck in front of his barn, where someone was sure to find him, and then she'd hike home. Gramps could take her back to town in the morning for her own car.

The rooster screeched.

Clanci jumped, then cursed. "Shut up," she said, more forcefully then she felt. "Look, bird," she said as she started the truck, "you just stay on your side of the seat, I'll stay on mine, and we'll both be as happy as two pigs in a produce store's garbage bin, okay?"

Henry glared past Jake at her.

❖————————❖

Five minutes later they were barreling down the highway toward Walker Acres when they hit a rut in the road.

Jake groaned as he bounced on the seat.

King Henry flew into the air, squawked loudly, then jumped to the back of the seat and began flapping his wings.

One wing smacked Clanci in the back of the head.

She batted at it with her hand as she tried to keep one eye on the road and the other on the bird.

Henry squawked even louder at being slapped. Half flying, half jumping into the front seat, he turned toward her.

Clanci's heart lurched. "Jake?" She held an arm up toward Henry to ward him off if he attacked, and tried to nudge Jake with her knee without taking her foot from the accelerator. "Jake?"

"Huh?" He sat up, looked around, then slumped against her, his head landing heavily on her shoulder.

The bird took a step toward them and placed a clawed foot possessively on Jake's thigh.

Clanci felt her heart nearly thump to a stop.

Jake placed his hand on her thigh. "Mmm," he sighed. "Nice."

She tried to push his hand away but failed.

King Henry puffed his chest, craned his neck, and let loose an ear-piercing crow.

Startled, Clanci nearly jumped through the roof of the truck.

Henry flapped his wings.

Jake's hand began to move caressingly up and down Clanci's thigh.

Heat shivers danced over her skin even as goose bumps of fear played a game of attack and invade.

Clanci rolled her window down. The air in the truck had become suffocatingly thin.

Jake's hand moved to the apex of her thighs.

She gasped and pushed back in her seat as a surge of something that felt all too much like fire roiled about in the pit of her stomach.

His hand moved with her.

She slapped at it.

Jake turned toward her, nuzzling his face into the crook of her neck. "Mmm, you smell so good," he muttered, his words slurred. His hand left her thigh and slid around her shoulders as his lips began teasing her neck.

A shudder of desire rocked her in her seat, and Clanci felt like screaming in frustration.

The headlights of an oncoming car suddenly appeared and nearly blinded her. She jerked the wheel to the right. The truck hit another rut, and she bounced off the seat, fighting with the steering wheel to keep the truck on the road.

A second later, as they sped down the road in full control, Jake's hand dropped from her neck to her breast.

"Jake, stop it," she spat out, and slapped at his hand.

He didn't notice. Instead, his thumb began to

play with her nipple, rubbing back and forth, back and forth.

The nipple instantly hardened. Clanci's heart-beat jumped into overdrive, and her breathing turned ragged.

She tried to push Jake's hand away again, then tried to push him away.

His hand dropped to her leg and his head lolled back onto the seat.

Startled, she glanced at him to assure herself he was still breathing.

A sort of soft, strangled snoring sound slipped from his throat.

A glance at King Henry found him glaring at her.

She turned her gaze quickly back to the road. The turnoff to the Lazy J loomed up out of the darkness. She slowed the truck to a stop and looked down the long drive. Both the main house and her cottage were still dark.

"Oh no," she said with a moan. Her grandfather wasn't back yet. She pounded a fist on the steering wheel. Her nerves were threatening to split apart into a million pieces. Why wasn't he back yet?

Maybe he got caught, a little voice offered from the back of her mind.

No. She rejected the thought. She wouldn't think along those lines.

King Henry clucked.

Clanci looked toward the houses again. If her grandfather wasn't back yet, then she couldn't take the chance of driving Jake home. They might run into each other, and Jake would find out that Harlen James had been trying to reclaim Midnight Blue.

Clanci steered the truck down the long, fenced drive and pulled to a stop in front of her cottage. This was not the way the evening was supposed to progress. In fact, lately she was having a hard time trying to figure out where her entire life had taken a drastic detour and headed toward doomsville.

King Henry suddenly screeched at the top of his lungs and flapped his wings.

Clanci flattened herself against her door.

Her dog, Buster, barked and jumped up at Henry's door, his claws scratching against the metal while his head bobbed in and out of sight.

The bird went into a frenzy of screams and began prancing frantically about on his scrawny legs.

"Whuh?" Jake struggled awake and grabbed the bird by his neck. "Stop!"

Henry squawked even louder as his wings flapped crazily.

Clanci grabbed the door handle and, jerking at it, practically fell out of the cab.

Buster instantly bounded around the truck. Fifty pounds of excited Irish setter jumped on Clanci, and before she could push him off, a huge tongue slid up one side of her face.

"Buster, stop!" she screamed.

"He just wants a little lovin'," Jake said, slipping his arms around her waist from behind and pulling her up against him. "Like me."

She hadn't even known Jake had gotten out of the truck. Straightening, Clanci started when she felt something hard press against her rear. Trying to pull away from him didn't work, so she twisted around. His eyelids looked so heavy, he appeared ready to pass out. No sooner had the thought taken form in her mind than Jake swayed against her.

"Okay, cowboy," she said, "I think you've had it for now." Slipping an arm around his waist and pressing her weight into him to keep him from falling, Clanci reached past him and slammed the truck's door closed.

She felt like sticking her tongue out at the rooster, who stood on the truck's front seat watching her.

Turning, she urged Jake toward the cottage. "Come on," she said, "slow and easy."

He grinned and flopped an arm over her shoulder. "My favorite way, sweed . . . heart."

She threw him a glower, which she realized he was too out of it to comprehend, then pushed open the door.

King Henry screeched.

Clanci glanced over her shoulder at the rooster while struggling to keep Jake upright as he slumped against her.

The bird jumped onto the truck's windowsill, flapped his wings, and dropped to the ground. Before Clanci realized what was about to happen, King Henry ran past her and into the cottage.

"No," she screamed after him.

"No, whad?" Jake echoed, his head jerking up. He grinned lopsidedly and pulled Clanci into his arms. "Didn't do nothin' yet," he mumbled, nuzzling her neck.

Sssssss!

Squawk!

Ahwooooo!

Meow!

Clanci jerked around and stared into the house as the sounds suddenly emanating from it grew louder.

Something crashed to the floor.

She jumped. Forgetting about keeping Jake steady on his feet, she pushed him away and ran into the house.

Jake fell against the doorjamb.

Clanci tripped over the shallow, bowl-type vase that had been on her coffee table, filled with wildflowers. The heel of her boot caught the wet, waxy leaf of a magnolia and slid out from under her as she flailed about trying to regain her balance.

Her rear end hit the floor with a loud thud.

Buster, tail between his legs and whining softly, scrambled under the dining table. King Henry continued to prance around the living room like a conquering soldier, and as Clanci struggled to a sitting position she saw Fluffles perched on a curtain rod over the couch, her ears flat, long black hair bristling, tail twitching, and green eyes glaring.

The blue curtains Clanci had hung only a month earlier now had claw marks up one side. The urge to murder something . . . namely a big, white rooster . . . ripped through her veins, and she knew counting to ten wasn't going to get rid of it.

Realizing she was sitting in a puddle of water from the vase, she started to get up and her gaze landed on her worktable across the room. It was lying on its side. The clay sculpture of Midnight Blue she'd been working on was on the floor, having landed headfirst.

King Henry pranced past.

"You monster," she snapped. She'd intended the sculpture to be a Christmas gift for her grandfather. Clanci got to her feet and, forgetting her fear of him, took a determined step toward the animal. "Roosters do not belong in my house."

At her advance the bird's wings flew outward, his chest puffed, he screeched at the top of his lungs, and he took a step toward her on one long-clawed, ugly yellow foot.

Clanci backed away hurriedly as Henry began to flap his huge wings furiously.

A loud thump sounded behind her. She spun around and saw Jake slumped precariously against the open front door, hanging on to the doorknob.

"I'll see to you later," she threatened the bird, and ran to Jake, slipping an arm around his waist just as he started to sag to the floor.

"Mmm, I missed you," he mumbled, and drew her to his chest. "Gettin' lonely."

She looked up into his eyes, wishing for a moment that he knew and meant what he was saying.

Then she reminded herself just who she was making that wish about and wondered if she'd totally lost her mind.

Ignoring the heat that had started to burn her body the moment he touched her, Clanci tried to push away from him.

Jake's arms tightened around her.

She turned her face away just as his head lowered toward hers. His lips grazed her cheek.

"Come on, Jake, you need to sleep it off." She guided him carefully toward a big overstuffed chair and pushed him down into it.

He reached up and grabbed her hand before she could turn away. "Not alone," he murmured, and pulled her onto his lap.

She collided with his powerful body. His strong arms wrapped tightly around her.

"Mmm, nice fit."

She tried to push away from him and felt hard, hot muscle beneath her fingers.

He nuzzled her neck.

"Jake." She shoved at his hands, which were beginning to roam, and half twisted, half leaped off of him.

He struggled out of the chair after her, staggered, and fell to one knee as he reached for her.

"You have a one-track mind," she said, slapping his hand away as his fingers grazed her pant leg.

He smiled. "Going your way."

She had never seen eyes so glassy.

He rose and stumbled toward her.

"No." Clanci grabbed his arm and spun him toward her bedroom. They staggered several steps together. "You need to sleep this off."

"With you," Jake said, turning to put his arm around her shoulders.

"Alone!" she countered, and pushed him down on her bed. The mound of lace-edged pillows that rested against the massive rough oak headboard of her bed flew to the floor.

"Mmm, this is good," Jake said, closing his eyes and letting out a long sigh as his body sprawled across the bed and his head sank into one of her goose-down pillows.

She looked at him for a long moment as he lay still. What would it be like, she wondered, to lie beside him, to let him hold her and make love to her? Half a second later, realizing where her thoughts had strayed, Clanci was so shocked with herself that her knees went weak and her hands began to tremble.

Grabbing the post at the foot of the bed, she backed away from him. "You . . . you relax," she managed brokenly, "and I'll . . . be . . . back in . . ." She swallowed hard. ". . . a minute." She moved on wooden legs toward the door, then turned to look back at him.

He hadn't moved.

A minute later he started to snore softly.

Clanci stood and watched him for a solid five minutes, part of her fighting to ward off the fantasies about him that were still floating around in her mind; another part of her still afraid he was going to up and die from the overdose of potion she'd given him; while still another part of her wanted nothing more than to make certain he was good and gone to sleepy-bye land before she made her next move.

How could she be attracted to Jake Walker? To *Jake Walker*!

She squeezed her eyes shut. She wasn't, she argued with herself.

Yes, she was, her conscience argued. And she had been ever since he'd moved to Coyote Bend.

She shook her head. No, she wasn't.

Yes, she was.

No, she wasn't.

Yes.

Clanci slapped a hand against the doorjamb and silently ordered her mind to stop trying to drive her insane.

"He's handsome," she said aloud to herself.

His black hair contrasted starkly against the whiteness of the pillow beneath his head. Her gaze dipped. Short curls of dark hair peeked from the open collar of his shirt.

The blood pounded in her temples and her cheeks began to burn. "Okay, he is sexy, in a rugged sort of way," she said, almost begrudgingly. "And maybe I've been lonely enough lately to find him physically appealing, but that's it." Anger crept back into her tone. "But he's a thief. An unscrupulous, low-down, lying thief."

Satisfied that she'd gotten herself under control

and that Jake was sleeping, not croaking, she stalked to her dresser, pulled one of the lower drawers open, and drew out several scarves. There was no telling how long he would remain asleep, and if he woke up anytime soon, there were two possibilities she'd rather not face. One, that he'd be more coherent and want to go home, which she couldn't allow. And two, that he'd kiss her again, which she *really* couldn't allow.

FOUR

Clanci tested the last knot and stepped away from the bed, satisfied with her handiwork. At least if he woke up now she would be safe, and he wouldn't be going anywhere.

The thought no sooner crossed her mind than Jake snorted and, in an effort to roll over, jerked on the scarves that held his arms and legs secured to the bedposts.

Clanci jumped back, stiff with apprehension, but he didn't awaken. When he finally did come to, she knew he'd be furious, but she'd deal with that problem later.

She walked back into the living room.

King Henry was perched on her coffee table, looking for all the world like Henry VIII sneering down on his subjects, except in this case one of his subjects was still cowering under the dining table and another was clinging to the curtain rod overhead.

As if trying to redeem himself somewhat, Buster crawled out from beneath the dining-room table and, hugging the back of Clanci's legs as his tail wagged furiously, looked up at her. The plea for help in his dark brown eyes was obvious.

She patted his head, then turned toward King Henry. She was an adult. He was just an oversized bird who couldn't even fly and had a brain the size of a pea. This was her house. She could do this. She sucked in a breath of courage. "All right, bird, it's time for you to go." She advanced on him. "Out!"

Henry instantly shot to his feet and turned to face her.

"Come on, out," she said again, and waved a hand at him in an effort to scare him toward the still-open front door. "Go. Go."

He crowed loudly and, puffing out his chest, flapped his wings.

Clanci stopped, afraid he was going to charge. Her gaze dropped to the long, ugly talons scraping the top of her coffee table, and she remembered the long scar that was still visible on her back.

She stiffened with anger and threw back her shoulders. "I will not be intimidated by a stupid bird," she muttered to herself. Glaring at him, she pointed to the door. "I want you out!" she said, raising her voice.

One spindly yellow foot rose and thumped back

down on the table, leaving an ugly claw mark on the wood's polished surface.

She fumed. Her father had made that table.

Another screech echoed through the house, and Henry turned his head so that one beady eye glared defiantly in Clanci's direction, as if daring her to come closer. He took a step toward her.

Clanci backshuffled furiously, nearly tripping over Buster. She hurried into the kitchen, Buster hugging her legs. "Some help you are," she snapped at the dog.

He rubbed his body against her thigh and looked up, his sad but hopeful eyes instantly making her feel guilty for taking her frustration out on him.

Clanci sighed. She hated roosters, had ever since she'd been six. Clanci shuddered just recalling that day. She'd wanted to see the newborn chicks, but the chicks' father hadn't exactly been endowed with a sense of hospitality. He'd gone after her like a bull after a red bandanna, and before she'd known what was happening, his claws had tangled in her long hair and his wings had slapped at the sides of her face.

After her grandfather rescued her, the doctor had sewn up the gash on her back and Harlen had killed the rooster, but Clanci had never ventured anywhere near the henhouse again.

She glanced back over her shoulder at the bird still dominating her living room, and tried to ignore the fact that her palms felt sweaty and her heart was doing wild somersaults.

She looked around the kitchen for something she could use as a weapon and finally pulled a large spatula from one of the kitchen drawers. It didn't feel big enough. She grabbed a huge cast-iron frying pan from the stove. Feeling a bit braver, she stalked back toward the living room.

Buster deserted her and returned to his hiding place under the dining table, wanting no part of a confrontation.

"Thanks, brave heart," she threw over her shoulders as she passed, then paused at the open door to the bedroom and looked in at Jake. He was still sleeping, and the scarves she'd secured to his wrists and ankles, hog-tying him spread-eagled on her bed, appeared secure.

Almost as if it had a will of its own, her gaze moved slowly over Jake. There was no denying, as far as looks went, he had it all.

Moonlight flowing in through one of the bedroom windows bathed him in a conflict of light and shadow that accentuated the rough-hewn curves and aristocratic lines of his face. His black hair glistened as if touched by a thousand stars, while his long, dark lashes shaded high cheekbones, and the barest touch of a smile on his lips hinted at tantalizing secrets.

Clanci felt an urge to touch him, to run her fingers through that thick mass of dark hair and feel it caress her skin, to slide her hands lightly over the long, rangy muscles so evident through the fabric of his shirt. The yearnings that had swept over her when he'd kissed her earlier suddenly returned, rolling over her like thunder over a meadow.

Buster whimpered, and Clanci instantly jerked out of the spell that had overtaken her.

If virility wasn't his middle name, then it obviously had to be trouble.

"Which is exactly what I'm asking for, standing here drooling over a no-good, lying thief like Jake Walker," she muttered. Setting the spatula and frying pan down, she stepped into the room to draw the curtains. She didn't know who'd be looking into her bedroom window, but she wasn't taking any chances.

At that moment King Henry shrieked loudly and charged at her from the shadows on the other side of her dresser.

Startled, Clanci screamed and jumped back toward the door. "What in blazes are you doing in here?" she demanded, her voice cracking with fear.

The bird walked toward the bed and, pausing in front of her nightstand, plopped himself down on the blue-and-white braided rug, as if daring her to come into the room again.

She backed out. "Fine. Stay there," she said with a growl, angrier than she could ever remember being. She stomped into the kitchen and retrieved Buster and Fluffles's food bowls from a cupboard. "What kind of man has a rooster for a pet anyway?" she grumbled. Reaching into another cupboard, she grabbed a can of dog food, then reached for cat food. "Stupid, that's what it is. Roosters aren't pets.

Dogs and cats are pets. Horses are pets. Even pigs and snakes can be pets. But not roosters."

Clanci set Fluffles's food bowl on the floor and called to her.

The cat scrambled down from the top of the curtains and crawled around the outer edges of the living room as she hurried toward the kitchen. A moment later Buster inched up to his bowl, but both animals were careful to keep one eye riveted on the bedroom door as they ate.

Clanci walked back into the living room and began to pace its small length. She glanced at the watch on her wrist. Her grandfather should have been back. She walked to the window and looked out into the darkness.

The barn stood like a huge hulking black shadow a little ways off to her left. The main house was to the right. Not a light shone in any of its windows.

Clanci stared at the old two-story clapboard. Four years earlier her parents had been on their way there when they'd gotten in a car accident. Clanci had been in her third year of college, but all she'd ever really wanted to do was live on the ranch and raise horses. After her parents' death she'd told her grandfather she wanted to stay. Never a talkative or demonstrative man, he'd merely nodded, but she had seen the gleam of happiness in his eyes.

Turning away from the window, and her memories, she picked up the remote control and clicked on the television, flopping down onto the couch.

How in the heck long did it take to steal back a horse anyway?

The beginning credits of a murder mystery appeared on the screen.

Clanci clicked it off. She might have enjoyed the show, but at the moment the idea of murdering Jake Walker seemed an all-too-inviting one, so she figured she didn't need any encouragement in that direction.

A soft snoring sound emanated from the bedroom.

This was all his fault. If he wasn't such a low-down, greedy creep, she wouldn't be sitting here on pins and needles, he wouldn't be passed out on her bed with his stupid rooster standing guard, and her grandfather wouldn't be sneaking around in the middle of the night trying to steal back their own horse.

She bolted off the couch and walked to the bedroom door. "Why did you have to come to Coyote Bend?" she demanded, glaring at Jake.

A soft snort strangled its way out of his throat, and he tried to roll over, but his bindings held him in place.

"Couldn't you have found a piece of land somewhere else to turn into your blasted dude ranch?" She smashed a fist against the open door.

The door slammed back against the wall with a loud thud.

Henry instantly shot to his feet and glared at her,

but Clanci was too busy fighting off the pain slash-
ing through her hand to notice.

The cottage was old, the doors solid.

Buster barked.

Clanci saw the dog standing at the front door,
and instantly forgot about the pain in her hand. She
ran to the window, hoping Buster was alerting her
to her grandfather's return. But beyond the window
the night was still and dark.

She opened the door and let Buster out.
"Grandpa?" she called into the darkness hopefully.
The only answer she received was the lonesome
howl of a coyote somewhere off in the distance. She
walked to the couch, flopped down, and clicked the
television on again. A commercial. She clicked from
channel to channel.

Clanci punched one of the pillows on the couch
and lay down again, not realizing until her head settled into the soft, goose-down folds just how tired
she really was.

But she was also too wired and worried over her
grandfather to relax. And sleep was out of the question. She stared at the ceiling, replaying the infuriating events of the past few weeks in her mind.

Why couldn't Jake Walker have stayed away?
She worried her fingers together. Why couldn't he
take no for an answer? Grandpa Harlen didn't want
to sell the Lazy J or any part of it, and neither did
she. It had been in the family for over one hundred
and forty years, and the fact that Jake had begun

sabotaging things after they'd turned down his last offer wasn't going to change anything.

Of course, they hadn't counted on Jake stealing their prize stallion.

Clanci rose, let Buster back into the house, and began to pace. Two years before a tornado had almost done them in. Swooping down on them with almost no warning, it had destroyed their best fields, taken the roof off the main house, and carried away three of their best brood mares. Without the stud fees they'd planned to get on Blue, they wouldn't be able to pay off the back taxes Gramps owed, let alone pay on the second mortgage they'd been forced to take out, or buy seed, or pay the workers. They'd lose the Lazy J. Clanci wasn't about to let that happen if she could help it, which was why, as much as she'd hated it, she'd gone along with her grandfather's plan.

A sound outside drew her to the window again, but it was nothing more than a jackrabbit skittering across her porch.

She resumed pacing. If Rick Murdock had been more of a man, *and* more of a sheriff, he'd have gone to the Walker ranch himself and gotten Blue when she'd told him what was going on. But he'd as much as called her a liar, and smiled while doing it, which shouldn't have surprised Clanci. The man was unbelievable. They'd dated a few times . . . before Alex. Two mistakes in her life she'd rather forget and couldn't, since both men lived in Coyote Bend and seemed to make a point of encountering her at least once a week. Rick had never quite been able to get it out of his head that she'd dumped him for Alex. As far as Clanci had been concerned, she and Rick had never been serious enough for either one of them to be "dumped."

"Rick and Alex." She snorted. "So much for my taste in men."

A strangling sound suddenly came from the bedroom, sharp and loud.

Startled, Clanci whirled around, afraid the overdose of Grandpa's potion was finally having some kind of adverse effect on Jake.

The moment she reached the doorway to the bedroom, King Henry charged from the shadows like a kamikaze pilot doing a death dive toward a battle cruiser.

Buster, at Clanci's heels, heroically barked at the huge bird and protectively stood his ground as Clanci shrieked and jumped behind the doorjamb.

Henry didn't flinch or stop. Instead, he flew at Buster, pecking him square on the nose.

Instantly losing his bravado, the dog yelped loudly and ran for cover, tromping over Fluffles on his way.

The cat emitted an ear-piercing screech as she tumbled across the floor.

Henry squawked.

Clanci grabbed a newspaper and threw it at him.

The paper opened in midair and sheets of it flew everywhere.

"Out!" Clanci yelled at the bird. "Out, out, out!"

"What the . . . ?" Jake lifted his head from the pillow and, feeling like the battle of the ages was going on inside of his skull, tried to look around.

Clanci, preparing to throw a magazine at the rooster, abruptly froze at seeing that Jake was awake. Her fingers tightened around the rolled magazine and every muscle in her body stiffened. The breath in her lungs stalled as she watched and waited.

He blinked several times in an effort to clear his blurred vision, then shook his head. Cannonballs instantly zoomed through his brain and crashed against his skull, land mines exploded, sending pieces of shrapnel tearing through what little coherent thought he possessed. Stars invaded this whir of pain. Jake groaned and sank back into the pillow.

How many blasted beers had he drunk?

Clanci waited, afraid to move, hardly daring to breathe. She prayed he'd fall back asleep.

"Damn, my head feels like the war of the worlds is going on inside it," he muttered a second later.

Clanci's hopes were dashed, and she bit down nervously on her bottom lip.

Fluffles curled herself around Clanci's leg.

Henry saw the cat and squawked.

"Shut up!" Jake bellowed, and winced at the sound of his own voice. He made a move to rise, and his right arm and leg jerked against the scarves holding him to the bedposts. "What . . . ?" His eyes shot open and a deep frown instantly marred his brow. He jerked his right arm again. Then his leg. Then his other arm . . . other leg. He raised his head from the pillow and looked at his feet.

Clanci took a step back, then another, until she was out of his sight.

Jake looked around the room. Where the hell was he? His eyes fell on the frilly curtains, the pile of lacy pillows on the floor, the oak dresser topped by what looked like a jewelry box, a couple of bottles of perfume, a silver hairbrush, and finally a framed picture of a young couple, a little girl, and an older man. Jake stared at the picture for several long minutes, trying to identify the people in it. Finally he realized that the older man was Harlen James, though at least twenty years younger than he was now.

Memory—or what there was of it—immediately returned to him. He yanked viciously on the scarves, jerking first his arms, then his legs. "Clanci!"

She jumped at the thundering roar of her name reverberating through the small cottage.

"You don't have to yell," she said as quiet again descended on the house and she stepped back into the bedroom. "I'm right here."

He raised his head from the pillow and pinned her with a murderous glare. "What's going on? Why am I tied up?"

Clanci tried to smile and failed. He seemed totally coherent, which meant Grandpa Harlen's potion had obviously worn off. "Well, you see, ah . . .

I didn't . . . I mean . . . you weren't . . . um, I couldn't . . ."

He suddenly relaxed and his glare turned into an arrogantly satisfied smile. "Oh, I get it." The smile widened. "But I didn't know you were into S and M, Clanci."

"What?" She stared at him, her mouth agape at the direction his thoughts had taken.

He shrugged a shoulder. "Well, I'll admit I've never tried it, but"—he glanced at the scarf binding one of his wrists to the bedpost—"since you've gone to all this trouble, I guess the least I can do"—the suggestive grin widened and a devilish spark lit his eyes—"is cooperate." He chuckled softly. "Unless I already have."

"That is not why you're tied up," Clanci said, her voice so affected by her surprise and outrage that the words came out of her mouth as little more than a gasp. "And nothing's happened!"

"Good, 'cause I'd hate it if I didn't remember being with you. Especially like this."

Fury swept through her. "Nothing happened and nothing is going to happen."

His smile instantly disappeared, and an icy coldness replaced the devilish spark. "Then why don't you explain just why I'm tied up."

She shook her head. "I can't."

"Clanci!"

Turning, she hurried back into the kitchen.

"Clanci, dammit, come back here and untie me."

She ignored him and began fixing herself a cup of coffee.

"Clanci!"

During the next fifteen minutes she heard almost every curse known to man, and learned just how fiery Jake Walker's temper could be.

FIVE

"Clanci!"

Jake yanked on the scarves, nearly dislocating his right wrist. He twisted his legs and cursed loudly. If it was the last thing he ever did, he would thrash Clanci James to within an inch of her life. He should have known better. Hadn't he learned his lesson with Katherine? Women who played hard to get usually ended up being a whole heck of a lot more trouble than they were worth. More challenging maybe, but definitely more trouble!

He jerked his right arm again. The scarf held and the skin of his wrist burned like crazy. What in blazes did she think she was doing anyway? All he'd done was kiss her.

Maybe she was crazy.

Jake jerked on the other bindings, then sagged into the bed. His wrists hurt, his ankles hurt, his head hurt, he was madder than spit, and his mouth

tasted like a hundred barefoot Indians had walked
through it.

"Clanci!"

King Henry bolted up from the rug, squawked
loudly, and began to prance around.

"Oh, shut up," Jake snarled at the bird.
"Clanci," he yelled again.

Henry's squawks and the sound of a television
set in the next room were his only answers.

Had she left? He called out again, with no more
success. He'd kill her. First thing. He'd put his
hands around her neck and . . . Jake thrashed violently, jerking every limb, twisting, writhing, and
bouncing.

The bedsprings squeaked, a pillow fell to the
floor, the spread rumbled into a ball beneath him,
and the posts shook, but his bindings remained secure.

A phone rang in one of the other rooms.

Jake stilled, listening.

Clanci grabbed the phone. "Hello?"

"Clanci, Blue wasn't in any of Walker's corrals,
but a couple of wranglers are nursing a brood mare
ready to foal, so I ain't been able to get a look into
the barn yet."

"Grandpa." She almost sagged against the dining table in relief. "You've got to come home." She
glanced over her shoulder toward the bedroom door
and lowered her voice to a whisper. "I've got—"

"Can't," Harlen said, cutting her off. "Haven't got Blue yet, but I will. Jake ain't on his way back here, is he? That'd mess things up."

"Well, he passed out, but—"

Harlen's cackling laugh momentarily startled her.

"Grandpa, it's not funny. I think I—"

"You gave him the powder like I told you?"

"Yes, but—"

"Good girl. Enough to keep him out of it for a couple more hours, I hope."

"Yes, but—"

"Good, good, good. Oh, something's happening."

"Grandpa—"

"One of the wranglers just came a-dashing out and is running toward the house."

"Grandpa, please, listen to me," Clanci said, her nerves strung so taut, she felt near to snapping apart. "Forget about that. Forget about Blue for now. You've got to come home. Please. I gave Jake too—"

"I ain't leaving here without Blue," Harlen growled. "And maybe a little extra for my durned trouble. Now stay put, girl, I gotta go."

"Grandpa—"

The click that sounded in her ear startled her. "Grandpa? Grandpa, answer me!"

Clanci pulled the receiver away from her ear and stared at it. He'd hung up on her. Panic niggled at the back of her mind and her heart nearly did a free fall into her stomach. Her grandfather wasn't even on his way home yet, and she had Jake Walker hog-tied to her bed.

"Damn!" She slammed the handset onto its cradle. What was she going to do? She could call her grandfather back and make him listen. She picked up the handset, but hung it back up almost immediately, realizing there was no way she could call him. If he was close to the Walker barn, someone else might hear his cell phone ring. It was a chance she couldn't take. Swearing softly, she stalked across the room and threw herself down on the couch.

"This isn't happening," she mumbled, closing her eyes and rubbing at her temples while she prayed she'd wake up any minute and find this whole thing had been nothing more than a very bad dream.

Buster crept up to the couch and laid his head across her knees.

She opened her eyes and looked down at him. "What am I going to do, Buster?"

He looked at her with his sad eyes.

A squeaking sound coming from the bedroom told her Jake was still struggling with his bindings. She winced, suddenly wondering which prison she'd be sent to after he had her charged with kidnapping. Would they charge her with assault too? Or attempted murder? A barely audible groan of despair slipped from her lips. Did they even parole kidnappers?

She bounced off the couch and paced, then walked to the front door, opened it, and looked out.

The darkness lay solidly over the landscape, weakened only by the pale glow of the moon and the light streaming out from her window. Other than the normal night sounds, all was quiet, Nothing moved to break the almost unearthly stillness.

A string of very unladylike expletives that she wouldn't dare mutter in front of her grandfather slid off Clanci's tongue in a harsh whisper. She slammed the door shut, then stomped to the dining table and sat down.

"Clanci!"

Jake's thundering roar cut abruptly through the silence of the cottage and nearly sent her through the ceiling. Scrambling for composure, she glared at the bedroom door. There was no doubt in her mind that Jake Walker was the absolute worst thing that had ever happened to her. Folding her arms on the table, she laid her head down on them. She felt like crying, but she was too tired.

A few minutes later Clanci woke with a start, instantly jerking upright. She glanced at the clock on the wall over the sink. Only five minutes had passed. She sighed in relief and rose. Walking to the counter and grabbing her cup, she poured herself another cup of coffee. She couldn't let herself fall asleep. That was the last thing she could afford to do.

What if someone came to the cottage? One of the fieldworkers or wranglers. What if Grandpa got caught trespassing and Barbara Walker called the sheriff? Rick would happily arrest Harlen in the blink of an eye, just to get a dig in against Clanci. And if he came to the cottage to talk to her, he'd see what she'd done to Jake.

"Clanci, blast it, answer me!"

She stilled. Maybe she ought to gag Jake too.

Jake waited several minutes for her to appear at the door. When she didn't, he cursed softly and stared up at the ceiling, visions of every torture device and technique he'd ever heard about dancing through his head. Tying her spread-eagled on the floor and slowly dripping water onto her forehead for about an hour sounded extremely satisfying. He could just imagine her writhing furiously in an effort to get away, her body twisting this way and that, straining against her bindings, against her clothes.

Suddenly the image changed. Clanci lay on the bed, spread-eagled and tied, and smiling up at him invitingly. Moonlight filtered in through the nearby window, painting her naked curves with its golden glow. Jake stood beside the bed, his fingers aching to reach out to her, every cell in his body hungry for her touch.

He shook his head and the image disappeared. But the fire that had ignited deep down within his body burned hot and sped through his veins, wild and uncontrollable, searing his flesh from the inside out. With it came an unbearable, gnawing ache of hungry desire that shocked him.

A groan rumbled from his chest. He barely stopped it before it slipped from his lips.

What in blazes was the matter with him? She'd drugged him, hog-tied him, and refused to tell him why, and he was fantasizing about making love to her? The realization stunned him. It was crazy. *He* was crazy. That was the only rational explanation. Whatever she'd given him had scrambled his brain. Made him temporarily insane. There was no other answer. Except that he'd secretly fantasized about making love to Clanci James from the first moment he'd laid eyes on her, almost nine months before. Not that there hadn't been a couple of other women in his life during that time. He was a man, not a monk. But he'd found out the hard way just what falling in love with the wrong woman could do to a man, and he wasn't too eager to travel down that road of disaster again.

Memories of Katherine momentarily filled his mind. She'd walked into his life like a vision, and he'd fallen for her, hard. The fashion model and the cowboy. Now it seemed as if everyone but he had known it would never last. Even Katherine. But she'd said all the right things, including "I love you," and he'd believed her. He'd told everyone else where they could put their opinions and concerns. Then Mr. Hollywood had shown up on the scene, and Jake's bubble had exploded like an A-bomb.

He opened his mouth to yell for Clanci again, but stopped before making a sound. Katherine had never yelled, never shown her temper, but she'd always gotten what she wanted. A smile, a few softly spoken words, and a sultry look in her eyes had worked like magic for her. He frowned. It had worked on him, so maybe he could make it work on Clanci. He cleared his throat, smiled, and called out to her in a deep, lilting drawl. "Clanci?"

She turned toward the bedroom, surprised that his summons was no longer a thunderous roar laced with fiery anger.

"Clanci, could you please at least come to the door?" Jake called again.

She bit her lip, apprehensive.

"Clanci? Please?"

His tone seemed velvet-edged, low, even seductive. Always too curious for her own good, she walked to the open doorway and looked in at him. The buttons on the front of his shirt had popped open during his struggles to free himself, so that now her gaze fell on a taunting view of sun-burnished skin and work-honed rippling muscle, covered by a sprinkling of dark chest hair.

She snapped her gaze away as her pulse instantly sped up. She swallowed hard and squared her shoulders. "Yes?" she said, trying to instill a chill into her voice and realizing immediately that she'd failed.

"Would you please tell me what's going on? Why have you got me spread-eagled on your bed and tied up like a sacrifice to the gods?"

She took a sip of her coffee and stared at him. If Jake Walker had any kind of honor or integrity, this whole situation wouldn't be happening. But he didn't. She could think of a hundred unsavory terms to describe him, but low-down, lying thief seemed the most appropriate.

"Whatever the problem," Jake said smoothly, "we could talk about it." He smiled. "Untie me, Clanci. I promise I won't try anything. We'll just talk."

She wasn't listening. Her gaze moved slowly over him, and in spite of the circumstances, she found herself appreciating what she saw. Physically, he was the embodiment of what she considered her dream man, consummately masculine, supremely virile, and so easy on the eyes, she could probably stand and stare at him for hours without blinking.

His hair was almost as dark as the night, and so rich that she knew each strand would feel like silk against her skin, while his amber-specked eyes were the most beautiful and mesmerizing she'd ever seen on a man. But it was his mouth, with that killer smile, that definitely deserved to have a warning label slapped over it.

Visions stirred in her imagination, a montage of fantasies she had no business giving thought to. Nonetheless they took form in her mind and sent little shivers of excitement coursing through her.

Jake tugged on one of his bindings, and Clanci jerked out of the spell she'd fallen under. Her appreciative stare instantly turned to a cold glare. He might be as handsome as sin and one of the sexiest men she'd ever encountered, but that didn't change the very real fact that he was also a lying, thieving jerk.

"Clanci?"

She started to turn away.

"Clanci, dammit, talk to me," Jake thundered, forgetting all about his resolve to remain calm and try to reason with her. He twisted and jerked against his bindings again.

King Henry squawked and bounded to his feet, prancing around the room.

Clanci gasped and jumped back.

"Tell me what's going on," Jake ordered, "or I swear, Clanci, when I get out of here I'll . . ."

She bristled at his threat. "You'll what?" she challenged, meeting his gaze. "Beat me up? It's about the only despicable thing you haven't tried yet."

"I don't beat on women."

"No, you just tear down their gates, cut their fences, set their haystacks on fire, and steal from them."

Jake looked up at her in astonishment. "What?"

Clanci glared at him. "Don't try to pretend with me, Jake Walker. This whole situation is your fault, so you've only got yourself to blame for being hog-tied and treated like the thieving creep you really are."

"All I did was dance you around the blasted dance floor at Sam's and kiss you," he bellowed.

"You came to Coyote Bend under false pretenses," Clanci countered.

"Pretenses?" He twisted furiously against the scarves. "I don't know what you're talking about."

"Liar."

"I am not a liar or a thief, but I'm beginning to think you're crazy." He twisted violently. "If you don't untie these blasted scarves, Clanci, I swear . . ."

She rammed clenched fists onto her hips and glowered at him, chin thrust out defiantly, her eyes shooting the sparks flaring through her temper. "You bought a ranch that only has access to the river by the easement across the Lazy J."

He stilled and pierced her with an angry stare. "So?"

"It's restricted to cattle use."

Jake's eyes grew darker. "So?"

"But you're not satisfied with that now, are you, Jake? You want more."

"I—"

"You want full access to the river. Unrestricted, so you can do anything you please, like ruin everything around here."

"You're crazy!"

"You're trying to force my grandfather into bankruptcy just so you can get your greedy hands on the Lazy J."

Jake thrashed against his ties. "I don't want the Lazy J."

"Oh, right." Clanci laughed insolently. "Tell me another lie, Jake. But this time try to be convincing."

"I knew it. You *are* nuts."

"And you're despicable."

"Maybe so, but I still haven't got the faintest idea what you're ranting about."

"Right. And this moon is made of green cheese. Save it, Jake, you don't lie very well when you're face-to-face with a person."

She turned away.

"Clanci."

Hair flying about her shoulders, she stalked back into the kitchen. Cursing under her breath for going to the door in the first place, let alone talking to him, she refilled her coffee cup. At the rate she was downing coffee, she wouldn't need to fear falling asleep; she'd be so full of caffeine she'd be bouncing off the ceiling.

"Clanci."

She ignored him.

Ten minutes later he was still calling her. Why did all the handsome ones have to be such jerks?

"Clanci, you're nothing but a coward."

She bristled. That did it! Slamming her cup onto the counter, she stalked back to the bedroom. "Coward?" she said, throwing him a glower that had made more than one man head for the hills. "You actually have the gall to call me a coward?"

"Tying up a man who's a little under the influence and accusing him of everything under the sun? Yeah, I'd call that cowardly," he said.

Clanci gritted her teeth and rammed both fists onto her hips. "Don't try to play innocent with me,

Jake Walker. I know exactly what you're up to, and you're not going to get away with it."

"I'm not up to anything."

"You tried that lie already."

"It's not a lie!" Fury echoed in his tone and shone from his eyes.

She snorted.

"Clanci."

"Where's Blue?" she demanded, throwing the words at him as if they were stones.

"Who?"

"Blue," she snapped. Her brows rose mockingly, and she cocked her head to one side. "My grandfather's horse, remember? The best stud in the valley? Chestnut? White socks? Sire of the last two Kentucky Derby winners?"

"How the hell should I know where your horse is? Don't you keep him in the barn?"

"Funny, Walker," Clanci said with a sneer. "Real funny."

"Untie me."

"Hah! Not a chance."

His angry gaze swung over her, arrogant and mocking. "What do you plan on doing, Clanci, keeping me here for the rest of my life?"

She shrugged. "Maybe."

"That's a hell of a long time, Clanci."

She tossed him a cool little smile. "Maybe. Maybe not."

SIX

Clanci stalked the living room from one end to the other. "Doesn't know what I'm talking about. Hah! Not a very convincing liar." She stopped, flicked on the television, instantly flicked it back off, and resumed pacing. "Maybe he should take lessons from Alex."

Buster, who'd finally crept out from beneath the dining table, lay on an oval braided rug before the couch and watched her pass back and forth in front of him.

Fluffles had curled up on a chair.

"Stealing a man's horse. In the old days he would have been hanged, no questions asked." She slapped back the curtain and glanced out into the darkness. "And I thought Alex stooped low. At least he doesn't go around stealing other people's horses. Women's affections, yes, but not horses." She smiled sardonically. "Obviously, Jake Walker doesn't have a conscience either. Trying to destroy an old man and take everything he's worked all his life for. Take his home."

Jake lay on the bed, trying to ignore the pain in his head and listening to Clanci grumble. He moved slightly and caught a glimpse of her as she paced back and forth across the living room.

It didn't take a genius to figure out that she was convinced he'd stolen her grandfather's horse. The problem was, he didn't know why she thought he'd steal Midnight Blue, or why he'd want the Lazy J. Hell, Walker Acres was all he could handle at the moment, and he was plenty satisfied with the way things were. He stopped struggling against his bindings and sighed. The only times he'd had any contact with Clanci in the months he'd lived in Coyote Bend had been at Sam's Bar & Grill, and a couple of times at one or another of the local stores. Every blasted time he'd asked her out, he'd gotten a cool rejection for his trouble.

She walked past the door again.

Jake's gaze moved to the sway of her hips.

She paused to look out the window.

The glow of a lamp on the table beside her touched the long tendrils of her hair, turning the red-tinged strands to silken waves of fire.

He lay still, watching.

Her body was a composite of subtle curves, with legs that seemed to go on forever and a waist that looked no wider than the span of his hands.

Want warmed his length and settled like a hot rope in his groin.

Clanci turned away from the window and caught Jake's gaze on her. She stilled instantly. No man had ever looked at her that way. At least not that she'd ever been aware of. His eyes seemed to be stripping the clothes from her body.

Her cheeks burned in remembrance of how she'd reacted when he'd kissed her. But it wouldn't happen again, she vowed. Cold indignation swept through her. Stalking to the door, she reached out to pull it closed.

"Clanci."

She told herself to ignore him. Instead she paused.

"You think I stole your horse."

It wasn't a question. She stared at him. His struggles had caused several locks of black curls to fall rakishly onto his forehead.

"Why, Clanci? Why are you so certain it was me?"

Even tied to the bed and obviously helpless, he radiated a virility that drew her. She steeled herself against it and gave him a somewhat contemptuous smile. "Why?" she echoed mockingly. "You really need me to list the reasons why, Jake?"

"Humor me," he said.

She rolled her eyes. "Oh, really."

"Humor me," Jake said again, his voice cold and demanding this time.

"Fine," Clanci said. "You've made several offers

on the Lazy J. When that didn't work, you tried causing a few accidents." A thin chill edged her words. "Nothing too major, just troublesome and costly. A cut fence here, a trashed gate there. But you obviously figured those tactics weren't working, which was right, so you decided to take things a step further and steal Blue." One red-brown brow arched upward. "Have I left out anything, Mr. Walker?"

A lethal coldness settled over his features. "I didn't do any of that."

"Right." She snapped the door closed and walked back into the living room.

"Clanci, I have to go to the bathroom," Jake yelled.

She snorted softly. He could call on every deceiving trick he could think of, but she wasn't falling for any of them.

"Clanci?"

Settling back on the couch, she grabbed a pillow and hugged it to her. "Grandpa, if you don't come home soon, I just might commit murder."

Ten minutes later she was asleep, her exhaustion winning over the caffeine.

Jake stared at the ceiling as every curse word he'd ever heard ripped through his brain. Jerking at the bedposts wasn't doing a thing except causing him pain.

At Clanci's terse explanation of what was going

on, his suspicions had jumped in a direction he'd rather they hadn't taken. But there was no help for it. Someone had attempted to buy the Lazy J and make it sound as if the offers were coming from him. Someone had caused some accidents around the place when the offers were refused, and now that same someone had obviously stolen the Lazy J's prize stallion. No matter how many times he went over the scenario, his conclusion was always the same; there was only one person who could make it look like he was the one responsible and gain by all of it.

"Barbara, if you're behind this," Jake swore under his breath, an image of his sister filling his mind, "that'll be it."

His half sister had been known in the past to be the cause of more than one problem in his life. Jake jerked on one of his bindings then turned sharply to look up at it. The movement sent pain spiraling through his head and crashing against his temples.

A few beers didn't cause that kind of a hangover, he knew, which could only mean that Clanci had spiked his drink with something.

When the pain began to subside, Jake opened his eyes and glanced toward the still-closed door. He'd been totally taken in by her flirtatiousness. Obviously one bad experience hadn't taught him anything. Maybe he really would be better off becoming a monk. Celibate and cloistered. At least then he'd be physically safe.

But even if Barbara had done everything Clanci

thought he'd done, including steal the horse, that didn't explain why Clanci had drugged him, brought him to her place, and tied him up on her bed. What was she doing, holding him for ransom? Jake almost laughed aloud. He might be Barbara's half brother, and in most respects they might be close, but if she was given a choice between him and a large sum of money, he had no doubt he'd come in a very sorry second.

Henry stood and flapped his wings.

"Oh, pipe down," Jake grumbled. He jerked his leg upward. Hope suddenly filled him as he felt his foot slip partially out of his boot. He relaxed his foot and twisted it slightly, then pulled upward. A smile broke over his face as his foot slid free. It wasn't going to get him off the bed, but it was a start. A minute later he had both feet free. He twisted around and looked at the bindings on his wrists. Scooting up toward the headboard he leaned forward and, closing his teeth over the knot of one scarf, began tugging at it.

A few long minutes later, panting, exhausted, and totally frustrated, Jake lay back against the headboard.

King Henry stood at the side of the bed, head cocked, staring at him.

"Yeah, I know," Jake mumbled, "it was a stupid idea."

The bird crowed softly and scratched at the rug with one foot.

Jake looked at the bird again and suddenly felt a

spurt of renewed hope. With his gaze darting between the closed door and the bird, he whispered,
"Henry, come here."

Henry looked at him but didn't move.

"This is not the time to get difficult or play
dumb, Henry." Jake growled, more than a hint of
menace in his tone. Why his late, amateur-magician
father had performed with a rooster in his act rather
than a rabbit or a dove, Jake had never understood.
And inheriting the beast had been something that,
up until now, he'd considered a curse. That hadn't
fazed Henry, however. Almost from the moment the
lawyer had said Randolph Walker's will declared
that his son, Jake, take over caring for King Henry,
the bird had attached himself to Jake like glue. No
matter where he went, Henry was at his heels, and if
he tried to leave him behind, the rooster put up such
a squawking ruckus that anyone within earshot usually threatened to shoot them both if Jake didn't do
something. That something usually meant giving in
to the bird's demand. Dates, however, usually failed
to appreciate Henry's company any more than Jake
did.

"Henry," he tried again, "come here."

This time Henry took a step closer to the bed.

Jake's gaze jumped to the door again and he held
his breath, dreading the possibility that she'd heard.
After a long moment passed and stillness continued
to hang over the house, he looked back at the
rooster. "Get up here."

Henry's head cocked back and forth several

times, then paused as one beady red eye stared at him.

Jack sighed in exasperation. This was going to be harder than he'd thought. Henry had been trained not to climb on furniture, though sometimes, when he went wild or became upset, he forgot that. Otherwise his manners were pretty good. At the moment, however, that was not something Jake was about to appreciate.

"Up on the bed," he ordered, his tone harsh but hushed.

Henry clucked softly and his head swiveled around so that he looked at Jake with his other eye now.

"Up on the bed, Henry," Jake said impatiently. "Now!"

Henry turned and walked away from him, not stopping until he was all the way across the room.

"Oh, blasted stupid bird!" Jake snapped. "Not that way."

Henry turned.

"Come on," Jake urged. "Over here. On the bed." He thumped a calf on the mattress as best he could and glared at the bird, praying he would follow his order, while at the same time wondering if there was a pan big enough in the kitchen at home to cook a twenty-pound rooster.

Henry shook himself, flapped his wings, and pawed at the floor with one taloned foot.

"You are not a bull, Henry," Jake whispered. "Now get up here."

Henry let loose with a garbled croak and ran toward the bed. A split second later he was in the air.

"Oh, geez." Jake grimaced and closed his eyes. Henry's feet landing on his thighs pierced the denim of his jeans. "Damn, Henry, get off," Jake said with a growl, wincing in pain as Henry flapped his wings and dug his talons farther into Jake's legs in an effort to balance himself.

The bird quieted and Jake moved his legs slightly, trying to dislodge Henry without sending him flying back to the floor.

Henry hopped off of Jake, nonchalantly walked to the end of the bed, and sat down.

"You're not done," Jake said. "Here." He wiggled his left hand. "Untie this."

The bird stood and moved curiously toward Jake's hand.

Jake held his breath and prayed Henry wouldn't grab hold of his arm. Barbara had been nagging him to trim Henry's talons after he'd put a scratch across her newly polished dining-room floor. Now he half wished he'd listened to her.

"Here, Henry," he prodded, "untie this." He wiggled his hand again, hoping the bird didn't mistake one of his fingers for a worm, and flipped one end of the scarf toward the bird. "Come on, you can do it."

Henry eyed the red wisp of material for what seemed to Jake an eternity, then finally pecked at it.

"Good boy," Jake whispered. "Keep going, Henry. Keep going."

Henry grabbed hold of the knot with his beak and viciously jerked and pulled at it.

Five long minutes later Jake's left hand fell free, and he silently thanked his father for training Henry to do everything from untying knots to riding a dog's back. He hurriedly twisted around and jerked loose the knot that bound his other wrist, then sat up and pulled his boots back on. Swinging off the bed, Jake got to his feet. His legs trembled, his knees buckled, and the room began to spin furiously. Cursing, he grabbed one of the bedposts to keep himself from sagging to the floor. The feeling in his legs and feet returned within seconds and the room stopped moving around him. But the throbbing in his head continued. Ignoring it as best he could, he turned and glared at the door. It was time to get some answers, and maybe teach a certain young lady that tying a man up could be hazardous to her health.

Not bothering with being quiet now that he was free, Jake stalked across the room and jerked the door open. His lips had just parted to growl out her name when he took a step, felt something under his foot, and an ear-piercing, heart-stopping screech filled the room.

Jake instinctively jumped back, stumbling into the door. "Geez, what the . . . ?"

A black blur of cat practically flew across the room.

Startled out of her sleep, Clanci's eyes shot open as Fluffles bounded across her chest and tore her way up the curtains. Waving her hands about in front of her, Clanci bolted from the couch and looked around wildly, trying to wake up, orient herself, and figure out what was going on. Her gaze stopped cold on Jake.

Nearly strangling on a gasp, Clanci whirled away from the couch. Tripping over Buster, she lunged toward a nearby corner of the room.

Jake's gaze darted in the direction she spun toward. "Oh, crap!" he muttered, diving for the same corner, and the old shotgun that lay propped up against it.

Clanci's hand wrapped around the gun's barrel.

Jake's strong fingers clamped down over hers, hard and unyielding.

"Let go," Clanci ordered, putting all her weight into trying to yank the gun toward her.

"No way," Jake snapped, jerking it out of her grasp.

Clanci lost her balance. Shrieking, she fell into him . . . hard.

He lost his grip on the shotgun when her arm rammed his, then lost his breath when her shoulder hit him square between the ribs. As air rushed from his lungs Jake grabbed her and stumbled backward.

The arm of the couch caught him in the back of the knees and he started to fall.

Clanci screamed, which caused Buster to sit up and howl.

Jake cursed, and King Henry crowed.

The minute Jake's back hit the cushions of the overstuffed couch, he rolled, pinning Clanci beneath him.

Holding her down, he rose slightly.

Clanci glared up at him. "Get off!"

He gasped for breath. "Tell me what the blazes is going on first."

"Get off or I'll scream."

One dark brow arched sardonically. "Go ahead. Who's going to hear you?"

Clanci let out a scream, and Jake winced as the dull throbbing that was still haunting the inside of his skull threatened to intensify.

"Stop!" he demanded, shaking her shoulders.

Clanci stopped screaming and shot him a withering glance. "Then get off."

"I will . . . after you tell me what's going on. What's been happening around here? And why'd you drug me and tie me up on your bed?"

"Believe me, that wasn't the way it was supposed to go," she spat out, momentarily numb with the shock that he'd managed to get free and turn the tables on her. "You are the last person I'd ever want in my bed, Jake Walker. I'd rather sleep with a rattler."

"Clanci, tell me—"

"You know exactly what's going on," she said, squirming under his weight. "You're trying to destroy my grandfather and get your hands on this ranch, and it isn't going to happen."

"I am not trying to get your ranch," he said, hard cold steel threading his voice and shining from his eyes.

Fury almost choked her. "Oh, and I suppose that real-estate man who was bugging us half to death with offers from you was lying?"

"Evidently."

"Liar."

His legs moved to straddle her as she tried to twist and writhe her way out from beneath him.

She stilled and graced him with a glare that he felt certain could frost the air. "I suppose all the things that happened around here after Grandpa turned down your offers were just accidents, right?"

"I don't know. Tell me about them."

"You cut our fences."

"No, I didn't."

"You set fire to some of our haystacks."

He shook his head.

"You destroyed several gates between the pastures."

"No."

"Yes, yes, yes, yes," she said. "And you stole Midnight Blue."

Jake felt his hold on his temper slipping, and his suspicions about his sister rising. "Clanci, you have to listen to me, I—"

"No." She twisted furiously, struggling to get away from him. "And if you don't get off of me, I'll have you arrested for assault."

"Have *me* arrested?" His hands pressed her shoulders down further into the cushions of the couch. "You're the one who kidnapped me, remember?"

"Only because you're a low-down, lying creep of a thief," Clanci said.

"I didn't make any offers on this ranch," Jake said.

"You can repeat that until the cows come home, Jake, and I won't believe you.

"Clanci . . ."

"My first impressions are usually pretty good, and my first impression of you was that you were a real jerk," she lied, wishing she could forget the fact that her first impression of Jake Walker had actually been to wonder what it would be like to be kissed by him.

"Fine, but not for the reasons you've—"

"You're going to go to jail," Clanci cut in. "I'll see to it, I swear, even if I have to go to the state capital and get the Texas Rangers involved. I'll get you arrested for stealing Blue, if nothing else."

"I didn't steal your horse."

"Oh yeah, right. He just vanished in a cloud of dust and a heigh-oh silver," she taunted.

His body was burning up. He looked at her lips. How could such a cantankerous, troublesome little spitfire be so damned beautiful?

"I didn't steal your horse," he said softly.

"Liar."

"About the only thing you haven't accused me of is murder," Jake said.

Her cool blue eyes fixed on him. "Maybe I haven't finished yet."

"Clanci, I don't know what's going on, but you've got to listen to me. I didn't—"

"Forget it. I'm not going to listen to anything you have to—"

With absolutely no thought to what he was doing, Jake's mouth swooped down upon hers, cutting off her tirade and capturing her lips as a predator captures its prey.

Clanci fought against him, trying to twist away, to move from beneath his weight, but her efforts were futile. He had her thoroughly pinned down. She was his prisoner. Yet the more she struggled against him, the more she realized she was fighting her own treacherous desires as much as she was him.

Excitement mingled within her anger, wicked and tempting, and inciting a fire of desire. His strong arms held her still against him, his hard body pressed into hers as his mouth assaulted her with a kiss that held more passion than she'd ever experienced in her life.

An unexpected surge of desire swept through her and ignited an ache in her loins that grew with each passing second that his lips continued to besiege her mouth.

His arms slid around her, one hand burrowing behind her nape and tangling within the long strands of her hair as he pulled her closer to him, pressing his tall, hard length into her body, deepening his kiss.

Clanci felt resistance swiftly slip from her body, and her mind.

His mouth moved over hers with a firm mastery that quickly drained away her anger, thoroughly banished her doubts. Need replaced everything she'd felt before, drawing her into its clutches, instilling her with a hunger of passion that was mindless, and causing her sanity to desert her completely. But if it was a warning, it went unheeded.

Seconds became an eternity. Time became meaningless, and with each caress of his lips, each stroke of his tongue against hers, she learned what it really meant to be kissed.

As her anger evaporated, her arms slipped around his shoulders, and the mutiny of her body was complete.

What he had intended to do, other than shut her up and cut off her accusations, Jake had no idea, but it didn't matter anymore. Overriding any hesitations he'd had about what he was doing was the pleasurable feel of the lips beneath his own, the lithe body his was pressing into, the long slim leg that had moved to entwine itself about his, and the small, hard breasts pushing against his chest.

A sliver of good sense still hovered at the back of his mind, like a specter of conscience, ordering him to let her go, warning him that what he was doing was dangerous. Clanci James was crazy. Volatile. Unpredictable. Fiery. Too independent. Stubborn. Self-righteous. All the things Katherine had been, and more. He should stop before it was too late.

But Jake wasn't listening to his conscience.

SEVEN

When he finally realized that she'd stopped resisting him and started responding to his kiss, Jake didn't know. He pulled away and, rising up on his elbows, looked down at Clanci.

Clanci felt her body tremble beneath his, as if his kiss, and then the desertion of his lips from hers, had ignited a rippling of aftershocks racing through her body. It was a wondrous feeling, and she knew it shouldn't be.

Her gaze met his, and she studied the lean, dark face hovering over her. A crooked smile lifted one corner of his mouth and the light in his whiskey-rich eyes burned like a steady flame as they seemed to probe her own.

She drew a long, shuddering breath. "We shouldn't have . . ." Her voice was barely more than a whisper; her words had a shaky uncertainty to them, and a slight catch in her throat prevented her from finishing the remark.

His handsome mouth twisted wryly. "Done that?"

Mesmerized, Clanci's gaze remained riveted to his as he lowered his head toward her and brushed his lips softly across hers.

A flash of passion danced in his eyes.

She turned her face away abruptly, knowing if she continued looking into his eyes, continued studying his face, any will she had left would abandon her completely. "Please," she said softly, "don't do that again."

He was silent and still for so long, she couldn't help but look at him.

A frown drew Jake's brows together, and his face seemed to harden.

The scent of the countryside clung to him; wild grasses, golden earth, worn leather, and summer nights. Beneath that was the redolence of his cologne, blending with the aromas of man and nature to create a fragrance that Clanci felt was distinctively Jake, and one she found surprisingly heady and somehow satisfying.

"Tell me what's going on, Clanci," he demanded softly. "When did all of this start? The offers? The sabotage attempts?"

As lightning snaps at the earth, cold reality snapped back to life within Clanci's mind. She was suddenly aware of the masculine force of him, of the power that dwelled within the corded muscles of his arms, the strength and purpose that seemed to fill the very air about him, and the will that shone from his eyes and emanated from his every move and word. He was her enemy, and she had succumbed to his seductiveness. Mortified, she pushed at his shoulders. "Let me up, Jake," she said, struggling beneath him.

He hesitated, measuring her reaction to his words. "Tell me what's going on," he repeated finally, making no move to release her.

Clanci drew in a long, ragged breath. Fury at her vulnerability to him, both physically and emotionally, roiled through her veins. It wasn't something she'd expected, and certainly nothing she welcomed. She'd rather be attracted to Frankenstein than to Jake Walker.

He saw the burning reproach in her eyes, but ignored it. "Tell me, Clanci," he ordered again, his tone laced with threat, "what's going on?"

She licked away the sudden dryness of her lips and tried to quell her building anger. The gall of the man, acting as if he were as innocent as a newborn lamb.

Jake found himself transfixed by the sight of Clanci's tongue moving slowly across her bottom lip. A surge of desire struck him, hard and low. He steeled himself against the needy response of his body. They'd already gone further in the last ten minutes than he'd ever intended, and though making love to the warm, lithe body lying beneath his was a pleasure he knew he would thoroughly enjoy, it was now time for answers.

"Since you're so fond of lying," Clanci said, her voice raspy from the conflict of emotions churning through her, "perhaps you should have been a politician."

She saw the cool sparkle in his eyes and suddenly wondered if she'd gone too far.

"I haven't lied to you, Clanci."

"Let me up."

"From what you've said so far," Jake said, ignoring her demand and propping his head on one hand, "someone's been offering to buy Harlen out."

She glared at him.

"And when that failed, they took to sabotaging things around here." He looked down at her. "Right?"

"You should know."

"And now your prized stud has been stolen, and for some reason you think I've done all of this."

"Yes." She slammed a fist into his shoulder. "And you're not going to get away with it," she said, twisting beneath him and shoving at him.

Jake pressed down on her until she stopped, but he was beginning to wonder if he was continuing to lie on her to keep her still so he could find out what was going on, or because he enjoyed it.

Twenty-four hours earlier the thought of lying on top of Clanci James would have been one he found more than tantalizing. Just an hour earlier, however, that same thought would have sent his

teeth gnashing and brought the word *never* screaming from his lips. But that was before her words had
taken his suspicions where he never thought they'd
go, and before he'd actually found himself lying on
top of her.

Clanci quieted again, panting for breath from
her brief moments of struggle.

"Now, let's continue," Jake said, smiling. He
saw that his calmness, and the fact that she hadn't
been able to escape him, had piqued her anger. He
ignored it, praying that wasn't a lethal mistake.
"The first thing we have to do is get your horse
back."

Disbelief swept into Clanci's eyes like a dark
cloud. "Fine," she said. "Where did you hide him?"

Jake frowned. "I told you I didn't take him."

Clanci smiled slyly. "Okay, so you had one of
your hired hands do it for you. But Blue isn't in your
barn or any of your corrals, so where did you hide
him?" She rolled her eyes. "Oh, excuse me. Where
did you have him hidden?"

"How do you know he isn't in my . . ." The
words died on his lips. Harlen. Jake inhaled deeply
and let the breath out on a long sigh. "Your grandfather is over at my place."

It wasn't a question, so Clanci remained silent,
not willing to verify anything. She squirmed beneath
him.

Her movement drew his thoughts away from
what might be happening at his place and back to

her. He looked down into eyes dark with reproach. "That's what this is all about, isn't it, Clanci?"

She stared at him defiantly.

"You wanted me out of the way so that Harlen could snoop around my place."

She remained silent.

"Right?" Jake demanded. His tone had turned harsh, and that gave Clanci a start, but she didn't answer.

"Right?" he growled again.

"Yes," she snapped, trying to wiggle out from beneath him again. "Grandpa's getting Blue back, and then we're going to make sure you go to jail."

"If he doesn't get himself shot for trespassing first," Jake said. "My sister has no compunctions when it comes to protecting what she owns." He swore softly. "How long has Harlen been gone?"

Breathless from her futile struggles, she thrust her chin up.

"Clanci, I'm trying to help you," Jake said, exasperation edging his tone. "I don't want to see your grandfather hurt. Now how long has he been gone?"

His words scared her into momentary compliance. "Since about nine o'clock."

Jake glanced at the watch on his left wrist. "Over four hours. What's taking him so long?"

"He hasn't found your hiding place yet." Rancor sharpened her tone.

Jake pushed himself off of her and rose. "I didn't steal your damned horse, Clanci." Glancing toward

the kitchen, where King Henry was pecking con-
tentedly at Fluffles's bowl of dry cat food, Jake
walked to the front door and jerked it open.

Clanci's heart jumped into her throat. He was
going after her grandfather. She couldn't let him do
that. Harlen might panic—or explode. She bounded
off the couch.

"Jake, wait."

"Henry, out!" Jake ordered, motioning at the
rooster to leave the house.

The bird instantly trotted past the door and disappeared into the darkness.

Jake slammed the door and turned back to her.
"I could go looking for Harlen, but I'm afraid if he
saw me he might make a grab for his shotgun, and I
don't especially relish the prospect of meeting my
Maker just yet."

"A little too hot down there for you?" Clanci
quipped, moving to stand before the rock fireplace
that spanned one wall of the room.

Jake's lips twitched with amusement as he
walked toward her. "Yeah, that's one trip I'm not
looking to hurry." He propped an arm on the rough
wood mantel and stared at her.

An invitation she'd rather not acknowledge
smoldered in the dark depths of his eyes. Her breath
caught in her throat.

"But back to the subject at hand," Jake said,
turning away and walking to look out the window.
"My ranch is large and there's too many places your
grandfather could be, especially if"—he turned back

to look at her—"as you say, Blue wasn't in my barn or corrals."

Disquieting thoughts and questions began to run through Clanci's mind as her cheeks burned. Was there even the slightest possibility they'd been wrong about him?

"Anyway, I doubt Barbara would really shoot at anyone. It might break one of her precious fingernails." He sighed deeply. "We should probably just wait. At least for a little while longer."

She remained absolutely motionless for a long moment, then crossed her arms and narrowed her eyes at him. "You lied."

He shrugged. "I stretched the truth a little to get you to open up to me."

Her blue eyes impaled him. She wasn't ready to believe anything he said, in spite of her body's traitorous reactions to him. "If you aren't the one behind all these things, then who is it?" Clanci said, challenging him. It was a dangerous move, but she was feeling desperate.

"That's what I've been trying to figure out, and I don't like the answer."

"Which is?" Clanci demanded.

He looked despondent. "There's only one other person who could benefit from getting your ranch."

Clanci's whole body stiffened with resentment. "I've known Tom Reynolds all my life," she snapped, thinking of the neighbor whose ranch bordered the opposite side of the Lazy J from Walker Acres. "If he wanted the Lazy J, he would just come out and say so, not use sneaky, underhanded tactics like you've been doing."

Jake stalked across the room, closing the distance between them until they were standing only inches apart. He scowled down at her. "I haven't been using any kind of tactics, and I wasn't talking about Tom Reynolds."

Her balloon of indignation instantly deflated. "Then . . . then who were you talking about?" she stammered. She looked up into his eyes. The move was a mistake. The air in the room suddenly seemed to disappear. "I'm . . ." She pushed past him and hurried toward her bathroom. "I'm going to take a shower."

Minutes later Clanci stood beneath the spray of hot water and felt its soothing effects relaxing the muscles in her shoulders, which had been tight and tense since the moment she'd left the house for Sam's Bar & Grill.

Why had she ever let her grandfather talk her into this foolish scheme?

By the time she stepped from the shower, the water had turned tepid, but she was so relaxed, she felt as if every muscle in her body had turned to liquid.

The ringing of the phone made her tense again. Half a second later Jake boomed out her name. Clanci jumped, momentarily disoriented, not knowing what or who had shattered the spell she'd been under.

The phone rang again.

"Oh. Grandpa." She grabbed a towel, wrapping it around her, and threw open the door. Running through her bedroom, she spun around the corner to the kitchen and dived for the phone. "Hello? Grandpa?"

"Yeah, it's me, girl. I checked their east pasture, but Blue ain't there."

She held the towel tightly around her. "Grandpa, listen to me. Don't hang up You've got to come home," Clanci said. "Please. We'll go to the sheriff tomorrow and—"

"Murdock? He couldn't find his way out of a box canyon, let alone find Blue."

"Grandpa, please, I—"

"I'm gonna check down by the river. You sit tight, and if that potion starts wearing offa Walker, you just give him some more, you hear?"

She glanced over her shoulder at Jake and gulped at seeing the way he was smiling and looking at her—like a hungry cat who'd just spotted a helpless mouse. She stiffened. Well, she wasn't helpless. She opened her mouth to tell her grandfather that Jake wasn't unconscious anymore, then thought better of it. Her grandfather would probably get upset and go off on a tangent. "Grandpa, please, give this up and come home."

"I'll be there in a while, girl. With Blue."

Clanci stomped her foot. "Grandpa, if you're not home in two hours, I swear, I'll go to the sheriff."

His chuckling was the last thing she heard before the click of the phone.

"Stubborn old man," Jake said.

She turned on him, fire in her eyes. "He wouldn't be doing this if you hadn't stolen his horse."

Jake sighed and settled into an overstuffed chair that faced the couch.

Clanci pulled the towel tighter around her.

Jake felt his insides contract and his body begin to harden. Obviously, there was something wrong with him. She'd given him nothing but trouble, and he was lusting after her. That made a helluva lot of sense. "I didn't steal your blasted horse," he snapped, upset with her as much as with himself. "And I'm getting more than a little tired of trying to convince you of that." He sat forward, hands dangling over his knees. "Clanci, think. If I had stolen Blue, do you think I'd just be sitting here now trying to convince you I'm innocent? Or offering to help?"

She tossed her head, sending waves of wet-darkened red-brown hair flying about her shoulders, and studied him with a speculative gaze. "I haven't heard any offer of help."

Jake settled back in the chair, raising one booted foot to rest on the opposite knee. "It's there whenever you need or want it, Clanci. Always has been."

Screams of frustration gnawed at the back of her throat while confusion swirled about her mind. Unable to remain still, especially under his constant scrutiny, she began to pace the room. They couldn't have been that wrong about him. She stopped and looked at Jake.

His gaze met hers, direct and open.

Clanci's cheeks suddenly felt as if they were on fire, and a perplexing crush of emotions settled onto her shoulders. Why was it so hard to think coherently when he was watching her? "You really believe your sister could be behind all of this?"

Jake shrugged. "I don't want to." On a deep sigh he closed his eyes and rubbed a hand over his face, then slid long, work-callused fingers through his hair. The incident in L.A. nagged at him. He looked back up at her a moment later, steel and disappointment clearly evident in his eyes. "But Barbara is nothing if not ambitious."

"But she's your sister," Clanci said, unable to believe he would actually side with her against his own blood.

"Barbara is my half sister, but that doesn't matter. What does is this situation, especially if she's responsible for it, and I can't deny that I've seen her be ruthless in the past when she's going after something she wants." He stood and crossed the room to stand in front of Clanci, effectively putting a halt to her pacing. "When our father died he left a pretty good-size estate, but neither of us was left enough to buy the ranch on our own, and that's what we both wanted. I'd had my fill of rodeoing, working cattle, and training other people's horses. Barbara hated her job with a Los Angeles public-relations firm and liked the idea of living in the country, especially if she could combine the experience with running her own business. The inheritance was our chance, but there was a problem."

She saw the troubled look that came into his eyes just before he turned away and walked to the window. Drawing aside the curtain, he stared out into the night for so long, Clanci thought he wasn't going to go on. She was about to say something when he spoke again.

"I wanted a working ranch. Cattle, pastures, breeding horses. The whole bit. Barbara wanted a dude ranch. Luxury and class in a cowboy setting. She had the contacts to make her ideas work, and I knew she had the brains. And I was confident about my plans, so we made a deal. We'd pool our money and make the ranch do both. I'd operate the working end, she'd operate the guest part." He turned back to face her, a hint of sadness etched in his handsome features. "I thought it was going pretty good"—he shook his head and ran a hand through his hair again—"but if she's behind all of this, then I guess I was wrong."

"For the sake of argument," Clanci said hesitantly, "let's say you're right, and I believe you." She smiled weakly, suddenly realizing how much she wanted him to be right, how much she wanted to believe him. "What do we do now?"

"Wait for your grandfather to come home. But first I'd appreciate it if you'd go put some clothes on."

His first comment surprised her, but his second

brought a burning flush to her cheeks. She'd actually forgotten she was standing in front of him with nothing on but a bath towel. Turning toward the bedroom, she paused at hearing Buster scratching at the door and whining frantically. She smiled weakly. "Poor thing always acts as if he's afraid I'm not going to let him back in." She hurried to the door and pulled it open just as a loud squawk split the peaceful night air and Jake yelled at her to stop.

But it was too late.

EIGHT

A whirlwind of fur and feathers suddenly filled the doorway.

Clanci shrieked and tried to step out of the way.

She was nearly trampled as Buster charged into the house, careening off of her right knee, while a flash of black cat streaked in between her legs. King Henry rushed in on the other animals' footsteps, squawking loudly and clapping his wings. One clipped Clanci's hand, while a sharply taloned foot tromped over her bare one and left more than one stinging point of pierced skin.

"Henry!" Jake yelled.

Squalling at ear-piercing level, the rooster chased after Buster.

Clanci screamed and limped after them.

A dining chair toppled noisily as Buster crashed past it and scooted under the table.

Fluffles made for the curtains and, momentarily confused out of her wits, raced up Jake's leg instead.

Jake bellowed as eighteen claws scurried up his pant leg. He grabbed the cat, stopping her before she made it to his chest, and unceremoniously tossed her to the couch.

Holding the towel at her breast with one hand, Clanci grabbed a magazine with the other and, brandishing it as a weapon, ran after Henry. "Get out!" she screamed, swatting at him.

Several white feathers flew through the air as he bounded across the dining area.

Jake lunged at him.

Henry evaded Jake and Clanci's efforts and ran under the table.

Buster let out a mind-shattering howl and, tail tucked between his legs, shot from under the table and ran into Clanci's bedroom.

Henry screeched and tried to follow.

Jake grabbed him by the throat and jerked him to a halt. "Stop!"

The rooster's feet slashed at the air as if he were still running, and a strangled squawk of protest gurgled from his throat.

Jake stalked to the still-open door, but instead of tossing the bird out, he gently set Henry down on the stoop, then hunkered down before him. The fingers encircling the rooster's neck opened and Jake began to stroke Henry's head tenderly. "You can't do that, Henry, may man," he said soothingly. "Now calm yourself down."

The bird cackled softly and shook his body, as if to force his ruffled feathers back into place.

Clanci watched in silent shock.

"Go on, Henry," Jake urged, "wander around outside for a while. It's okay."

Henry cocked his head, clucked softly, and thrust a beady red eye at Jake, who rubbed a finger soothingly up and down the rooster's long neck. "Outside," he said again.

The bird turned and walked into the darkness. Jake rose, closed the door, and turned back to Clanci. "Well, that was exciting."

"I doubt Buster and Fluffles would agree with you," she said, then in spite of herself she saw the humor in the situation and burst out laughing.

Jake glanced at the cat, who'd found her perch on top of the curtain rod, then looked past Clanci into her bedroom. Buster was nowhere in sight. "Yeah, I guess not," Jake said. "Henry can be a bully sometimes."

"Sometimes?" she said, still chuckling.

In spite of his smile, Jake looked chagrined. "Okay, he's a bully all the time."

She knew she shouldn't ask but couldn't help it. She was dying of curiosity. "Why do you . . ." Clanci paused, suddenly not sure she should go on.

"What?"

She thought she saw laughter in his eyes, and that encouraged her. "Why do you have a rooster for a pet?" Clanci said quickly before she could change her mind. "I mean, you have to admit, it is rather unusual. Most people have dogs, cats, horses, even pigs."

"He belonged to my father," Jake said, before she even finished. "They were partners."

His words startled her. "Partners?" she repeated, trying to keep her mind on the conversation. The magnetism of his smile seemed to reach out and touch her, making her feel suddenly warm all over. She swallowed and tried to hold on to her train of thought. "Your father and a rooster? And he gave the bird to you?"

"My dad was a magician. Worlore the Wonder."

Her brows rose in surprise. "Worlore the magician is your father?"

"He was," Jake said, nodding.

"I've heard of him. He's been on television."

"Quite a few times, actually."

"Yes, I remember. I saw him on a variety show once, and he was on some Christmas special last year." She laughed, finally remembering his performance. He used the rooster instead of an assistant. "He's wonderful."

"He died last year."

Clanci saw the fierce pride that had filled his eyes while they'd talked of his father, and suddenly, for no explainable reason, she knew she wanted to believe in Jake Walker. It was ridiculous to change her feelings so abruptly, and for a reason she didn't even understand herself, but there it was. That simple. Maybe she was wrong, maybe she'd regret it, but she wanted to believe in him, and she was going to try. She felt suddenly as if a great weight had been lifted from her shoulders. Whatever had happened, whoever had sent the offers for the ranch through that slick-talking, city-polished, out-of-town real-estate agent, whoever was behind the sabotage efforts at the ranch and the theft of Midnight Blue, she felt certain, for the moment at least, that it wasn't Jake.

Thankfully, her grandfather wasn't around to ask for her reasons. She chased the thought away and smiled. "Would you like some coffee?"

A long sigh slipped from Jake's lips, and closing his eyes, he rubbed at them with his thumb and fingers. "I thought you'd never ask."

Clanci's smile turned to a frown at realizing how bloodshot his eyes were. "Is something wrong?" She bit down on her lip, not wanting to admit to having drugged him. "Do you have a headache or something?"

"Yeah. Whatever it was you slipped into my drink at Sam's, its aftereffects are still banging around in my head like a marching band."

Her mouth dropped open in surprise. "You knew I . . ."

Jake smiled. "Not until you just admitted it."

She shook her head. "I didn't mean to hurt you, Jake, or even knock you out. It was only supposed to quiet you a bit. Make you more . . ."

Jake saw the turmoil in her eyes, heard the remorse in her tone. The urge to pull her into his arms was almost overwhelming. But he had a feeling this wasn't the right time—wasn't sure there ever really would be a right time for them—and he wasn't at all certain that was a bad thing. Earlier Clanci had reminded him of Katherine. That was something he definitely didn't like, and something he wasn't sure he even wanted to deal with.

He steeled himself against the urge to drag her into his arms, telling himself it was a physical need, not an emotional one. Clanci barely believed him, was just now showing the faintest inclination to trust him, and to resolve this situation with her grandfather and the ranch, he needed to keep her that way. "We've still got a while to wait for your grandfather," he said, "if he doesn't show up before your deadline."

He looked up and caught her watching him, some indefinable spark of deep emotion shining in her eyes.

His mind didn't recognize it, but some inner, primitive instinct obviously did. The pain of his headache was suddenly forgotten as his body began to harden. He hurriedly took a seat at the dining table as she placed a cup of coffee and two aspirins in front of him. She straightened, realizing she had yet to put on any clothes. "I . . . ah . . . better get dressed."

Jake downed the aspirin and took a gulp of coffee. "Yeah, you'd probably better."

A few moments later she returned to the table and sat down across from him. A worried frown pulled at red-gold brows that curved delicately above her blue eyes. "Grandpa won't come back without Blue."

Jake crossed his arms in front of him on the table. She'd drugged him, shanghaied him, and accused him of being a thief—and he still wanted to make love to her. The feeling was so strong, the need so deep, there was no way he could deny it. He was obviously crazy. "Tell me again what's been going on, Clanci," he said, in an effort to get his mind back on business. "Start with the very first thing that happened, tell me everything, and don't leave anything out."

She gave a curt nod of consent and indulged in a long sip of coffee before beginning. "It started only a few weeks after you moved onto the old Banstell property," Clanci said.

Jake sat quietly over the next half hour while she talked, but she didn't miss the anger that came into his eyes, or the resignation that seemed to weigh down his broad shoulders.

"I can see why you thought it was me," he said when she finally finished.

Earlier that night she would have been convinced he was the best liar in the entire country. Now she felt certain she and her grandfather had severely misjudged him. Unless she was the world's crown fool, a possibility she still couldn't rule out, she had been more totally wrong about Jake Walker than she had been about anything or anyone in her life.

She suddenly wanted the conversation off of her and her problems, but more than that, she wanted to know more about this man she'd exhausted so much energy disliking, and who now seemed to attract her so thoroughly. "Let's take a break from all that for a while," she said, forcing a lightheartedness into her voice she didn't really feel. "Your turn. Why did you stop competing in the rodeo?"

He looked surprised. "How did you even know I did? It's not like I won a championship or anything."

"I was married to Alex Tremaine."

"So I've heard."

She wondered what else he'd heard but decided not to ask. "Alex considered everyone his competitor," Clanci said, "and he made it a point to know the name and standing of every cowboy in the business, whether they were on top, bottom, new to the business, or on their way out." She shrugged. "I guess it rubbed off."

Jake smiled. "Well, I'd broken just about every bone in my body I could break, made a little money, and had a few laughs. It was time to move on."

"Ever married?"

"No."

The curtness of his answer, along with the layered, dark look that swept over his face, surprised her, and for the briefest of moments a chilled silence seemed to settle over the room. She sensed there was more behind his answer and was just about to open her mouth with another question when he cut her off.

"I understand you're a veterinarian."

She smiled. "I graduated from the University of California at Davis with a degree in veterinary medicine, but I've never actually worked at it."

"Why not?"

She shrugged. "Grandpa needed help with the ranch after my parents died."

"And you couldn't do both?"

"I thought about it. But Coyote Bend already has one good vet. There's no need for another."

"Things change. People like a choice. Anyway, you could always set up somewhere else."

All of her doubts and suspicions about him suddenly came flying back into her mind. "Is that your way of making another offer on the Lazy J?" she asked coldly.

"I never made one, so I couldn't make another," Jake said easily. "I thought you were finally starting to believe me on that."

Clanci nodded, but in spite of herself, she couldn't quite banish every wisp of suspicion from her mind. "Forget I said that. More coffee?" she asked, smiling and rising from the table.

"Yeah, sure."

She grabbed their cups and walked to the counter. Glancing back at him over her shoulder as she poured the coffee, she saw him rub at his temples. "How's your headache?"

He opened his eyes and looked up at her. In the midst of trying to keep his mind off the idea of dragging her into his arms and making mad love to her, and of finding out exactly what had been going on to convince her and Harlen James that he was a low-life thief, he'd forgotten all about having a headache. "Almost gone," he said, happy to realize this was at least half-true. The banging drums and cymbals were gone, but they'd left behind a dull ache that seemed to have settled in his right temple.

Clanci placed their coffee cups on the table along with a plate of pastries she'd taken from one of the cupboards. She resumed her seat across from him and her gaze settled on his mouth as he raised the coffee cup to his lips. From the moment she'd walked into the bar and grill earlier that evening and centered her attention on Jake Walker, she had felt trapped within a war zone of battling emotions. Part of her insisted he was good, that he was telling the truth. He was innocent. But another part of her kept whispering that she was being fooled.

He wasn't the type of man she had ever wanted to get involved with. In some ways he was too much like Alex, in other ways he was not like him at all. But it was the small similarities she found between the two men that frightened and unnerved her. She knew her heart couldn't take another wound like the one Alex had inflicted.

But Jake's kiss haunted her every thought and move. She couldn't get the memory of it out of her mind. Worse, she couldn't forget how it had made her feel. It had stirred emotions in her that Clanci had been certain Jake Walker could never stir. She'd disliked him . . . had felt she was safe around him . . . and she'd been wrong. But the thing that unsettled her even more was something she wished she could deny: She wanted him to kiss her again.

Her gaze moved upward, and she caught his eyes searching her face, as if attempting to delve further and discover her secret thoughts. It was unnerving, yet exciting. A gnawing ache of desire invaded the pit of her stomach, and try as she might, she couldn't banish it. Her hands trembled slightly as an image of herself wrapped in Jake's arms flashed through her mind. She cupped her fingers around the hot mug.

Jake smiled. He had been watching the play of her emotions flitter across her face, wondering at each. She intrigued and attracted him, but he sensed she wasn't the type of woman who could accept anything less than a total commitment. She would want it all, and he wasn't certain he could offer her that much of himself.

Clanci tried to relax by pulling her gaze from his and turning it toward the window and the twinkling stars nestled in the black sky.

Getting romantically involved with Jake Walker would probably be one of the worst things she could do. Maybe he hadn't sabotaged the ranch or stolen Blue, but that wasn't the whole of it. Coyote Bend was a relatively small town, and people talked. Especially about newcomers, and Jake would be a newcomer until he'd lived in the valley for at least ten years or more. Rumor had it that he'd been quite a womanizer while following the rodeo circuit, just like Alex. And she'd heard he'd already started dating several local women.

"A penny for your thoughts," Jake said.

Clanci stared at him.

He smiled, while light smoldered within the amber specks in his eyes.

A warning voice whispered in the back of her head. She'd gotten too comfortable with him. Told him too much. Let her guard down. "You wouldn't get your money's worth," she said finally.

Jake instantly sensed the change in her demeanor and wondered at it. "Try me."

Her mind spun. "I was just worrying about my grandfather," Clanci lied, suddenly feeling chagrined that she hadn't even given a thought to Harlen James for the past forty-five minutes.

Jake nodded. "Yeah, well, he should be back pretty soon." He stood and walked to the living-room window, pulling back its curtain and looking out. "Why didn't you and your grandfather go to the sheriff when the sabotage incidents started?"

"Rick Murdock and I aren't exactly on the best of terms," Clanci said.

Jake turned and threw her a puzzled look. "Oh?"

Clanci wished she'd thought of some other excuse for why they hadn't gone to the sheriff and had decided instead to take the law into their own hands. It would sound so arrogant, trying to explain that

Rick Murdock was a Neanderthal who still held a grudge against her because she'd married Alex. "It's a long story," she said.

Jake walked back to the table. "Well, we've evidently got a lot of time."

NINE

Just beyond the hills in the distance beyond the Lazy J, the afternoon sun began a slow descent, allowing a smattering of shadows to creep back over the land. Its golden rays filtered through the small windows of the cottage and painted the living room in a haze of shimmering light.

The soft sounds of the country day struggled against the approaching silence of evening.

Buster, feeling the need to go outside, nuzzled his cold nose against Clanci's hip.

She grumbled a soft protest against waking up and, turning on her side, snuggled deeper into the warm cushion beneath her head.

Jake's arm tightened around her shoulder as Clanci's hair brushed lightly across his chin. He shifted position on the couch and one booted foot slid off the ottoman it had been propped up on. It crashed to the floor with a reverberating thud.

Clanci bolted upright.

Jake's eyes opened slowly and he looked up at her. "Good mornin'," he drawled lazily.

She stared down at him. What was she doing? Why was she on the couch with him? And how had she come to be sleeping in his arms? She pushed herself up and stood, then brushed a nervous hand over her wrinkled shirt.

Sunlight flowed brilliantly through the windows.

She absently swept a hand through her tousled hair, trying to remember what had happened, trying to orient herself to the situation.

Buster nudged her again and trotted to the door.

Her body felt tired and heavy. She stretched her arms, bent over to stretch her back and legs, then straightened and moved to open the door for Buster. Halfway there she stopped dead in her tracks as her gaze fell on the clock on her kitchen wall. "Oh no," she said with a moan, "it can't be." Jerking back the sleeve on her arm, she stared at her watch. "This is impossible. How could we sleep nearly the whole day away?" She looked at the window again, at Jake, at the clock, her eyes wide with alarm.

Buster whined and began a little doggy dance before the front door.

Jake unfolded himself from the couch, mumbled something she didn't quite catch, and walked to the door, opening it for the dog and then looking across the wide yard toward the main house. "Damn." He squinted against the glare of the sun. "What in blazes time is it?"

"Four-thirty," Clanci snapped, irritated with herself, her grandfather, Jake, and the entire world at large.

He turned to look at her. "You check to see if your grandfather came back while we were sleeping?"

Almost before he'd finished asking the question, Clanci pushed past him and ran toward her grandfather's house. "Grandpa?" She bounded up the wooden stairs. "Grandpa? Are you here? Grandpa?"

The screen door slammed behind her and she paused in the large, old-fashioned kitchen. A chill hung over the room. The old, percolator-type coffeepot was empty, the huge, white stove cold.

"Grandpa?" She ran toward the stairs to the second-floor bedrooms. Maybe he was asleep.

"He's not here," Jake said, walking into the house behind her.

She stopped, halfway up the stairs, and whirled to face him. "How do you know?"

"I checked for his truck."

Clanci raced back downstairs, through the kitchen, and out the back door. "Something's wrong. I know it," she threw over her shoulder. "I have to go find him. He could be lying hurt out there somewhere." She didn't want to think of the possibilities, but she couldn't help herself. Anything could have happened. His horse could have come up lame, or worse. He might have been bitten by a snake, fallen and hit his head, or broken a leg.

Jake grabbed her by the arm before she was halfway across the yard and forced her to stop. "We'll both go."

She looked up at him, wanting to trust him and still not sure she could.

The ringing of the phone in her cottage broke the spell that held them both momentarily still.

Clanci jerked her arm from Jake's grasp and ran to the cottage. She tripped over Buster's rubber dog-bone chewy just inside the door, half ran, half stumbled across the room, and grabbed the phone from its cradle just as it stopped ringing. "Grandpa?" she gasped into the receiver.

The dial tone droned in her ear.

"Damn." She slammed the handset back onto its cradle and turned to glare at the dog chewy.

Jake walked into the cottage, the expression on his face questioning.

"He hung up," she said. Walking across the room, she picked up Buster's chewy and threw it through the open door.

The phone rang again.

Clanci spun around and dived for it. "Grandpa?"

"Yeah, girl, it's me," Harlen said. "You okay, honey? You sound kind of funny."

"I'm fine. I was just up checking the house for you. Where are you? I've been worried sick. Why haven't you come home yet?"

" 'Cause they moved Blue before I could get to him, that's why," he growled, sounding for all the world like a man ready to take someone's head off.

"But I know where those buzzards have taken him and I'm gonna—"

"No, Grandpa," Clanci said hurriedly. "Listen, please, you can't do anything more. You have to come back. We'll go to the sheriff. Jake will—"

"I ain't going to Rick Murdock! Good-for-nothing bag of wind is all he is." Harlen spat, nearly blasting her eardrum into oblivion.

"But, Grandpa, we can—"

"No. Now you listen, honey. I'll have Blue in just a little while and we'll both be home. You sit tight and don't do a thing, you hear? Not a thing!"

"But—"

He was gone.

Clanci cursed softly and slammed the handset back onto its cradle again. Why didn't her grandfather ever listen to her? She turned and began to pace the kitchen.

"You're just like your grandfather," her mother had always said. "Impulsive, opinionated, and very stubborn." The words echoed in Clanci's mind. It was true, she and Harlen were very much alike, but each of them had their own views of how things should be done too. That led to some very heated discussions between them, since he never listened to her, and she rarely listened to him. Her grandfather had warned her against getting involved with Rick Murdock, and he'd warned her against marrying Alex. She hadn't listened either time, and both relationships had ended up a disaster.

On the other hand, he hadn't listened to her

when she'd advised him to breed Blue to their own brood mares before putting him up for service, or when she'd advised that they have Blue insured. He'd also rejected the idea of buying another stud, insisting that they couldn't afford it.

Now, if her grandfather didn't get Blue back, they might lose everything. Even if he didn't and they somehow found a way to pay off the back taxes, get the mortgage payments up-to-date, and keep the ranch, they'd still be finished in the horse-breeding business. People reserved stud service months, sometimes a year, in advance, and last-minute cancellations were costly. The Jameses would never be trusted again.

"I take it he's still not ready to come in?" Jake said, breaking into her thoughts.

She turned to see him standing in the open front doorway, one shoulder leaning against the doorjamb. There was something lazily seductive in the stance, and in the way he was watching her. It both excited and aggravated her. "No," she said, deciding aggravated was definitely the safer way to go. Reaching for the coffeepot on the stove, she filled it with water at the sink.

"So, what's the plan?" Jake asked.

She set the pot back on its electric plate, filled its top cup with fresh coffee grounds, and turned the unit on before turning to face him.

The afternoon sun was already dropping out of the sky and its waning golden light fell across his wide shoulders and danced off of the silver conchos attached to the hatband on his Stetson.

For a split second she felt so overcome by the world and all its real problems, she wanted nothing more than to throw herself into his arms and forget everything but how good leaning on him, borrowing some of his strength, would feel.

Clanci stiffened against the thought. One time in his arms, one time feeling his lips on hers, had been enough to warn her that he was much more dangerous than she had ever anticipated. He was a temptation she would do well to resist. And at the moment she wasn't at all sure that her earlier feelings of wanting to believe in him, to trust him, hadn't been merely a result of total exhaustion and the undeniable but infuriating attraction she felt toward him.

"Did he say where he was?" Jake said, breaking into her thoughts again.

She stared at him. Her grandfather had seen Blue at Walker Acres. All of her suspicions about Jake returned twofold. How could his sister steal a horse and hide it on their ranch without him knowing about it? "Yes," she said softly. She started toward the bedroom, intending to change from the clothes she'd had on all night into something not quite so rumpled. Her face ached for a splash of water, her teeth screamed to be brushed, and she had no doubt her hair probably resembled a wild mane of tangles.

Jake pushed away from the doorjamb.

Clanci stopped, warning bells going off in her

head. He wasn't tied up anymore. She had to be careful. Stay calm. Keep him there, but not too close. The doorway to her bedroom loomed huge in the corner of her eye. Her nerves jangled. "Ah, the coffee should be ready in a minute."

He moved across the room toward her.

She spun around and zipped back into the kitchen. "Why don't I get our cups ready? Would you like some toast, Jake? I'm afraid I don't have any more pastries." She grabbed a loaf of bread from the fridge.

"Toast is fine."

"I have some cereal and canned peaches," she added, knowing she was rambling but unable to help herself. She pulled them from a cupboard. "Or I could scramble us a couple of eggs. Frozen waffles. I have those too. Oh, wait, you probably want something more, huh? Steak?" She began rummaging in her freezer. "I think I have one in here someplace."

"Toast is fine," Jake said again. "Where's Harlen?"

"He'll . . . he'll be back in a little while," she said. "Would you like some orange juice?" She dived into the refrigerator again.

"Mind if I use that shower of yours?" Jake said, running a hand through his hair.

Clanci straightened and looked past the refrigerator door at him. "Ah, no, sure."

He turned and walked into the bathroom.

Pouring the orange juice into two glasses, Clanci considered sneaking over to the main house while

Jake was in the shower. Her grandfather's quieting potion was in a little bottle in his desk. If Jake was asleep, she wouldn't have to worry about him leaving. Even though he knew her grandfather was at his place looking for their horse, she couldn't take the chance of letting Jake go. What if he was lying to her? What if he went after Harlen?

She overpoured one glass and juice spilled onto the counter. Clanci reached for a dish towel.

Jake opened several drawers and a cupboard but couldn't find her hair dryer. Wrapping a towel around his waist, he walked into the living room.

Clanci was busy at the kitchen counter, her back to him. "Clanci, I can't find your hair dryer."

"Oh." She turned. "It's—" Her mouth dropped open. A rainbow of emotion flashed through her eyes in a millisecond as her gaze raked over his chest, glistening with silver drops of water nestled amid short, silky curls of black hair.

Friendliness. Warmth. Surprise. Appreciation. Desire. Clanci felt her blood begin to boil and fought against the feeling. He was the enemy, and in spite of what he said, or what she felt, until she knew otherwise she had to keep believing that. She had to. All the warmth left her eyes, and as she stiffened, a dark coldness invaded her body.

Jake's brow drew into a deep frown. She kept changing on him, and he couldn't figure out exactly why, but he had no doubt they were back to being adversaries. At least from her point of view.

And that was the last thing he wanted. There

had been plenty of other women in his life—seductive ones, beautiful ones, classy ones—but none had affected him so instantly, so thoroughly, as Clanci had. But considering what had transpired over the last twenty-four hours, he should want nothing more than to be as far away from her as he could get. He should label her crazy and forget about her. But he couldn't. He didn't know what it was about Clanci James, what there was about her that pulled at him, drew him, obsessed him, but he couldn't deny it, and the strange thing was, he didn't want to.

Even while some nagging little voice in the back of his head kept yelling out a warning to him, reminding him of Katherine, of the disaster that relationship had turned into, his mind and body filled with the desire to pull Clanci into his arms and smother her lips with his. And, after all, it wasn't as if he were considering proposing marriage to her.

"I didn't steal your horse, Clanci," Jake said softly. He pushed away from the doorjamb and moved across the room toward her.

Clanci cringed against the counter at her back, seeking escape and fearing there was none.

"I didn't set your haystacks on fire." His hand came up, and the tips of his fingers softly caressed the line of her jaw.

"I didn't cut your fences."

His eyes seemed filled with deep longing, while the heat of his body, so close to her own, reached out to envelop her.

"Or tear down your gates." His thumb moved

tenderly over her bottom lip, a featherlight touch that sent shivers racing up and down her spine.

Her fingers dug into the counter's edge and for a timeless second her gaze searched his face. Her limbs trembled and tingled with a warmth that pulsated through her entire body. She stared into his eyes. "How can I believe you?" she asked, her voice raspy with emotion.

Jake's arms slid around her waist. "I don't want your water," he said huskily. His lips brushed across hers.

Clanci felt the traitorous yearnings she'd been trying so desperately to deny threaten to ignite into flame. A shiver of anticipation—or fear—rippled its way slowly up her back. Just as abruptly, every nerve in her body became deathly still. Her heart seemed to pause in its erratic beat, and the breath in her lungs refused to move either in or out of her body. She was suddenly unable to breathe, to look away, or to resist him.

"I don't want your ranch," Jake whispered as his lips moved down the long curve of her neck and, like fire sweeping across a prairie, left a trail of flame in its wake.

A faint rush of sound caught in her throat. Hot tears stung the back of her eyes, and her hands moved to settle on his arms in a halfhearted attempt to push him away.

"I don't want your horse," he whispered huskily against her throat. His arms tightened around her.

Clanci's heart thumped erratically.

He pulled her up against his length, crushing her body to his. The corners of his mouth curved into a slight smile that deepened the hollows of his cheeks and the carved lines that framed his lips.

"I only want you," he said, and his lips captured hers.

TEN

The heat of his hands on her back seared through the thin cotton threads of her shirt, pressing into her, crushing the soft contours of her body to the hard lines of his.

Longing and desire flamed to life within Clanci's blood. She should pull away, fight him, resist him. He wasn't the man she wanted. She couldn't trust him. He was too much like Alex. But pulling away from Jake, moving out of his arms, abandoning his kisses, was the last thing in the world Clanci wanted at the moment.

The touch of his lips on hers, so warm and exquisitely gentle, sent a shiver of desire skipping through her body, assaulting her senses, routing her hesitations, and momentarily banishing her doubts.

His hands pulled her closer and pressed her body into his until she felt she had never been as close to any man.

Suddenly she knew this was what she had wanted from the first time she had seen Jake, all those long months ago. She had denied it to herself, refused even to consider the possibility, and yet somewhere, in the dark recesses of her mind, she had always known.

His hand caressed her back, his touch a fiery flame, burning into her flesh, branding her.

She felt his fingers move to bury themselves within the thick waves of her hair. Her arms slid around his neck, holding him to her, even as she knew she should push him away. A trembling weakness spread through Clanci's body as his mouth devoured hers in a kiss that was as gentle as it was demanding, as unhurried as it was seeking. An explosion of feeling erupted within her, volcanic and consuming. She twisted her mouth away. "Please . . . stop," she said with a gasp, dropping her head, unable to look at him, and shaking it as she pushed at him to release her. She knew that at any moment, if he continued this deliciously ravaging assault of her, she would lose herself to the swirling ache of desire that had attacked her the moment his lips had claimed hers.

Jake stilled.

"I can't . . . I'm sorry . . . I can't . . . do this," she whispered, her tone laced with anguish. She kept her eyes averted from his, refusing to look at him, too afraid that if she did, the last threads of the willpower she was clinging to would instantly desert her.

She glanced quickly toward the door, hoping someone—anyone—would come walking through it and stop this insanity she'd plunged into. Yet at the same time she was terrified that someone would do exactly that.

Jake stood still, watching her but not totally releasing her. A soul-bending desire gripped every fiber of his being. It urged him to ignore her protests and reclaim her lips, drag her back up against him, and make her want him as much as he wanted her. Instead he merely continued to hold her.

He felt the shiver that raced through her, saw the soft hint of pink that swept across her cheeks, and the slight quivering that attacked the lips he found so irresistible.

She was as vulnerable to his touch as he was to hers. The thought set off a savage need in him, a need to hold her close and protect her. He didn't understand it, but at the moment he knew he didn't have to. His arms tightened slowly around her, drawing her back to him. When she didn't resist him, satisfaction, and a kind of quiet relief and joy, swept quietly through him.

He heard her breath turn ragged as she rested her face against his chest, heard the slight catch of breath in her throat as he lowered his head and pressed his lips to the smooth skin at the curve of her neck.

"Why have we been fighting this, Clanci?" Jake whispered against her skin.

She felt her cheeks turn to fire at the touch of his kiss.

The scent of her filled his senses, while the taste of her honeyed flesh on his tongue aroused hungers within him that left him trembling with need.

"Jake," Clanci whispered, part of her pleading with him to stop, the other part begging with him not to. Passion consumed her. It clouded her brain, assailed her every thought, engulfed her entire being within its fiery flames. She was losing control, had already lost control. Whether he was her enemy incarnate, or the realization of every fantasy lover she had ever dreamed about, she didn't know, but at the moment the ability to care was swiftly deserting her.

His mouth moved to cover hers in a kiss that threatened to touch her soul and make it his.

Reality suddenly spun out of her grasp and time ceased to be. Nothing mattered anymore except the madness swirling through her senses, the soft caress of his lips upon hers, the desire coiling like a knot deep inside of her.

He was her darkness and light, her reality and fantasy. Reason, common sense, rational thought all spun away from her universe as longing seized her body and left her with no other thought than to belong to this tall, dark stranger who had so ruthlessly invaded her world.

Yearnings long buried swept through her, feelings long denied assaulted her and flew free. Desire flooded her veins, her senses, every cell of her body, every breath she labored to pull into her lungs.

Haunting little warnings danced about the edges of her mind, beckoning her toward caution, whispering of dangers beyond belief, and she ignored them all. He was the lover she'd been waiting for all of her life.

Jake's body was steel hard with the devastating hunger that had been ripping through him from the first moment he'd dragged her into his arms. He wanted to feel her lying beneath him, naked, hot with passion, aching for his touch as badly as he ached for hers.

His mouth caressed hers tenderly, elicited her acquiescence, and demanded her surrender.

A soft moan escaped her throat as her body betrayed the last vestiges of her sanity. Her resistance was vanquished, her doubts and hesitations momentarily forgotten. His tongue was a dart of fire, probing fiercely, burning her wherever it touched, stoking her own passions until she thought she'd go mad. Desire of a strength she'd never felt before flowed through her veins, filling her body with fire, inciting it with need.

Clanci told herself she should pull away from him, even as she knew that was the one thing she couldn't do. She had waited for him for too long, dreamed of him too many times to deny herself the ecstasy of him now.

His lips left hers to move gently along the curve of her jaw.

The pleasure igniting within her was explosive

and total, arcing through her like a bolt of electricity.

His tongue traced the line of her neck and his lips pressed into the small hollow at the base of her throat.

The weakness of ecstasy seized her, and she leaned into him, needing the bulwark of his length as well as his strength. Her entire being trembled with the force of the pleasure his caresses had aroused within her. She felt her knees tremble as his lips once again descended upon hers, and his body enveloped her within a blanket of desire. Her body quivered at each new touch as she returned his kiss with reckless abandon.

Control was something she had never let slip from her grasp, defeat something she'd never given in to . . . but she did now. Both slipped from her as swiftly and quietly as the waves do from the distant shores. Words she had never uttered to any man slipped naturally and comfortably from her lips. "Love me," she whispered softly against his mouth; pleading, demanding. "Love me."

Jake pulled back, leaving her feeling suddenly more alone and lonely than she had ever felt in her life.

Clanci saw the surprise of her words in his eyes, but she also saw his hunger, the loneliness that matched her own, and the passion that screamed not to be denied. There were no more doubts in her mind, no more hesitations or resistance. "Make love to me," she said again, and reached up to draw him back into her arms.

Crushing her to him, Jake smothered her lips with his, his tongue delving into her mouth to ravage it with a devastating sweetness.

He felt his mind and senses swirl as she responded with all the fervor of a starving lover. The hunger in his body was near overwhelming, and building with each caress of her tongue, her hand, her breast. Coherent thought had all but left him. Only the realization that he wanted her, more desperately than he'd ever wanted any other woman, was left in his mind.

Without taking his lips from hers, Jake lifted her into his arms and carried her into the bedroom.

Like something out of a dream, the room was awash in the hazy golden light of the setting sun and the dusky shadows it left behind.

She pulled him down with her when he bent to lay her on the bed. The need within him grew hotter, more demanding, more savage as their bodies entwined and her tongue dueled with his, teasing him, tempting him, daring him. A delicious sense of excitement assailed Jake, turning his body to steel and his blood to a rapturous fire that threatened to devour him.

Their clothes were a barrier Jake could no longer tolerate. He needed to touch her everywhere, feel her bare flesh pressed to his, slip his hands over skin he knew would feel like silk. Forcing himself to tear his lips from hers and move from her embrace, he pushed off the bed and stood.

Clanci's eyes opened at once and she looked up at him, her lips passion-swollen, her arms suddenly feeling empty, her heart afraid.

"Are you sure about this?" he asked huskily, not knowing how he'd survive if she said no.

Clanci nodded.

Relief whipped through Jake and a crooked smile pulled at one corner of his lips as he bent toward her, took both her hands in his, and drew her to her feet. Without a word he slipped his fingers beneath the buttons of her blouse and, his eyes never leaving hers, flicked each button loose, then pushed the blouse from her shoulders and let it fall to the floor.

Hungry gnawings of passion twisted like a knot in his groin as his gaze moved over the curve of her shoulders and down to the soft swell of her breasts, kissed golden by numerous days beneath the sun. The long tendrils of her red-tinged brown hair caught the last rays of the daylight flowing through the bedroom windows and turned to a fiery halo, while dark flashes of desire danced within the midnight depths of her eyes.

He reached out tentatively, afraid she'd change her mind and tell him to stop, terrified he'd suddenly wake and find himself alone in his own bed, and everything that had happened between them— was happening between them—was nothing more than another dream.

His index finger slipped beneath the hook of her

brassiere. He pushed it apart with his thumb and forefinger and the delicate lace-trimmed silk slid away from her.

Another wave of desire sliced through him, sharp, hot, and instant, like a streak of lightning. He stood motionless, mesmerized by the sight of her, his need for her deepening with each passing second, a torment to his soul that was both sweet and unbearable in its growing intensity.

Her eyes beseeched him to touch her, to love her, but she made no move.

Jake watched her breasts rise and fall with each breath she took. Finally he could stand it no longer. He raised his hands and cupped her breasts, one in each hand.

A soft moan slipped from Clanci's lips and her legs trembled, threatening to buckle beneath her weight and cause her to sink to the floor.

Jake felt a weakness invade his own limbs as his fingers curled around the soft, silken flesh.

She leaned toward him, slipping her arms around his neck as her nipples hardened into small peaks of need.

His mouth closed over hers and he slid her jeans over her hips, feeling them tumble down the length of her legs until finally settling on the floor. All the while her tongue continued to dance a seductive gambol around his, and the thought flashed through Jake's mind that if he was dreaming, he never wanted to wake up.

As her curves tucked neatly into his hard contours, Jake's hands explored, lightly tracing a path over her exposed back, traveling the soft lines of her waist, the subtle rounding of her hips, the tight contour of her buttocks.

His lips traveled, too, following his hands, marking new trails of their own, cutting new paths. Then he stopped. As his breath came labored and hard he stared at her as if unable to believe what was happening between them, or even that she was really standing there before him, naked and wanting him to make love to her.

Suddenly, feeling his gaze move over her, Clanci experienced a wash of abrupt and intense modesty and embarrassment. Quickly raising her arms across her breasts, she started to turn away from him.

"No," Jake said, stopping her with a gentle touch of his hand to her arm.

She paused and looked up at him, uncertain.

"You're so beautiful," he said, his voice rough with feeling, even more so than he had imagined. He let his gaze move over her again, slowly tracing each perfect curve and line, the very act deepening the hunger that was clawing at his insides, heightening the anticipation that coiled hot, tight, and demanding within his gut.

It was hard to breathe. His throat was so parched, his mouth so suddenly dry, he could barely swallow. With a groan of need stronger than anything he'd ever felt, he dragged her back into his arms, capturing her lips, stealing the breath from her lungs.

Clanci shivered as the passion of his kiss played havoc with her senses, and his tantalizing caresses worked to destroy whatever remaining vestiges of doubt, hesitation, or resistance might still be lurking deep within her. Yet she desperately needed more. She slipped her arms from around his neck, deserting the spot where her fingers had reveled in twining about the shaggy locks of his dark hair.

Her hands dropped to his chest and, twisting her lips away from his, she pushed him away.

ELEVEN

An involuntary groan ripped from Jake's throat. He stared down at her, confused, hopeful, yet full of despair as a silent scream of denial shagged through him, ripping at his insides. A frown drew at his brow as a shadow swept over his eyes, chasing away the warm amber lights and leaving only darkness. His lips parted as he prepared to ask what was wrong.

A Cheshire cat smile pulled at Clanci's lips as she reached out to place a finger to his lips. "My turn, cowboy," she said huskily.

Realization and delight instantly brightened Jake's eyes, and his face split into a wide grin as the shadows that had drawn at it only seconds before disappeared. "My pleasure, lady," he drawled, spreading his arms in welcome.

Beyond the small windows of her bedroom, night was steadily descending upon the land. It settled about the base of the trees, invaded their limbs, swept through the wild grasses that covered some of the hills and pastures, and finally seeped quietly into the small cottage.

For a brief moment Jake and Clanci stood unmoving in the waning light as it danced within the dark curls of his hair like twinkling stars and bathed her body in varying shades of burnished bronze and milky magnolia, depending on where it touched.

Jake ached to bury his hands within the wild mane of her hair, press his body against the tantalizing length of her naked form, run his hands over every curve and line. But he remained still, barely daring to breathe, letting her have her way with him, and afraid if he made the slightest move, the barest sound, she would disappear.

With one smart tug, she freed every pearlized snap on his shirt, then pulled the tails of his shirt from his pants and slid her hands under the fabric. She smiled at his sharp intake of breath when he felt her hands pushing the garment from his shoulders and trailing down the sinewy length of his arms. Tingles of excitement danced over her body at the feel of hard, ropy muscle beneath her fingers, and though she relished the power that emanated from him, she luxuriated in the shudder she felt rip through his body at her touch, testimony of her own power over him.

Her fingers skipped lightly over his rib cage, played with the faint sprinkling of dark hairs on his chest, then dropped suddenly to the silver belt at his waist. She released the clasp of his jeans and pushed the zipper downward. She heard his breath turn ragged and felt his body jerk in passionate reaction.

Her slow, sensuous seduction of him was almost his undoing. Jake clenched his teeth, hard, then his fists, closed his eyes, and struggled to maintain control of his body.

Smiling to herself, Clanci bent and, with teasing slowness, pushed at the jeans that hugged his hips and long legs so tantalizingly.

Jake's heart hammered wildly against his chest, explosive, painful thuds that threatened to burst free from his flesh at any moment. Her hands moving slowly back up his body, each touch a daring taunt, was a physical torture more delicious than anything he had ever known.

Clanci straightened then, but as Jake's arms moved to encircle her and draw her close, she backed away.

"Not just yet, cowboy." With a wicked smile on her lips, she let her gaze move over him as wantonly and slowly as his had moved over her only moments earlier.

He was perhaps the most perfectly built male she had ever seen. Or maybe she thought that at the moment only because she wanted him so badly, her pulse was racing nearly out of control and her heart was threatening to just up and stop.

His body was long, hard, and lean, his flesh golden perfection. *Rugged* was definitely the word that described him.

There had been other men in her life, handsome, thoroughly virile men, but she knew now that none possessed the untamed, almost feral masculinity she sensed in Jake Walker. It seemed to emanate from him like an invisible mist.

Closing the distance between them, she held his hands still while she pressed her lips to the center of his chest, then to the hollow of his throat, then, standing on tiptoe, kissed the curve of his collarbone.

A growl of need ripped from his throat.

Clanci's right hand deserted his. A second later her fingers invaded the dark thatch of hairs at the juncture of his thighs, and closed swift and sure around his arousal.

Jake nearly dropped to his knees as shock, hunger, desire, and need assaulted him with heart-stopping force. Passivity and inaction had never been his strong points. Tearing himself away from her, he struggled to remove his boots and socks, kicked his jeans across the room, then swept her into his arms and down onto the bed. His mouth claimed hers in a kiss that demanded her unconditional surrender while giving up everything he had to offer. His tongue plundered her mouth, raped her senses, explored her sweetness, and incited her passions.

She felt something hot and vital begin to build deep within her, and curled her body into the curve of his. Boldly she began an exploration of her own, her hands moving over every part of his body that she could reach; his back, neck, shoulders, arms, slipping into the dense curls of his hair and reveling in the sensation of silk slipping through her fingers.

Jake's body felt as if it were burning up, as if his skin had turned to fire, and her hands were stoking the flames, searing through him wherever they touched, through flesh and muscle, and even through his bones. All his past vows to be more cautious and protect himself deserted him as if they'd never existed, as did the pain, the worries, and the fear.

Whatever had happened in the past was over and done with. Memories of Katherine, of her arrogance and deceit, no longer mattered, no longer existed. His awareness now was only for the woman in his arms, the bewitching creature whose very taste and feel was driving him mad with need.

She had become his world.

Clanci knew she was on the verge of losing all thought, of being capable of nothing more than feeling, experiencing, reacting to the pleasure and hungers his touch was inciting within her. Yet she was also almost overwhelmingly conscious of everything about Jake Walker—the faint hint of leather and horseflesh that clung to him and slipped through the cologne of spices he wore to tease her senses like an aphrodisiac, his hard, well-honed chest, so disturbingly hot as it crushed down upon her breasts, and his long legs entwined so intimately around her own.

She felt his hands on her breasts, her hips, her thighs, moving everywhere, drugging her senses, teasing her with a touch here, a provocative caress there. She responded to each stroke of his hands with wild abandon and an ardent recklessness that would have surprised her—if she had been able to make herself think about it. But she was beyond thinking.

Jake's lips moved from her mouth to her neck, along the curve of her shoulder, then his head slowly lowered and his lips settled upon one breast.

Her breast surged at the intimate touch that sent currents of need racing through her.

He drew its nipple into his mouth with tantalizing possessiveness, gently sucking and teasing with his teeth, caressing the hard little peak with his tongue.

Clanci felt her consciousness ebb and spark as her senses reeled, as if short-circuited. A moan of pleasure ripped from her throat and her body instinctively arched up to meet his touch in a silent plea for more.

The moment his mouth returned to hers, Clanci's tongue dived between his lips like a flame desperately seeking sustenance, darting crazily, dancing seductively.

Every thought left to him fragmented as her body beguiled and ravished his. He drew her closer, pressing her into him, feeling the passion pounding through his veins, through hers. Every touch of her tongue, of her hands on his body, of her breasts rubbing against his chest, left him seared and hungrier for her than he had been just the moment before.

She was his prisoner . . . he was her captive. Conqueror and slave . . . slave and conqueror . . . they were both.

He had made love to more women than he could remember, his days on the rodeo circuit one of highs and lows, parties and one-night stands. Katherine had made him want more, and then shown him just how vulnerable his own heart was. But even Katherine had never made him feel the way Clanci was making him feel. He had been with Katherine for over a year, but she had never touched him as deeply, as thoroughly, as Clanci had in only a few short hours.

Clanci felt passion pound through her blood, through every pore of her skin, as his hands explored her thighs, then moved to her taut stomach before slipping down toward the red-gold curls of hair at the juncture of her thighs. The tips of his fingers brushed over the sensitive flesh that harbored her most intimate secrets, her most intense desires. Clanci tightened her legs instinctively, trapping him there as her body exploded in a series of blasts of pleasure so powerful, so intense, that she cried out his name, over and over.

But the exquisite torture didn't stop. She gasped in sweet agony, whimpered into his kiss at the delicious torment. With each touch of his fingers, each light caress, each subtle stroke, another onslaught of pleasure ripped through her, leaving her hungry for yet another . . . and another.

She wanted him, needed him, more than anything she'd ever needed or wanted in her life. It was as if he were the reason behind the very breath in her lungs, the beating of her heart, the impetus for the blood to flow through her veins.

He shifted his weight over her then, urging her legs apart with his, whispering in her ear, dragging his lips down her neck, holding her tight.

Then he was inside of her, filling her.

Clanci cried out, the pleasure pure and explosive. Her body instantly molded itself to Jake's, their passion-sensitized flesh fusing together, holding tight.

Jake breathed deeply of the sultry scent that was Clanci James, a blend of woman and jasmine. He pressed his lips to her throat, traced the curve of her earlobe with his tongue, and buried his face within the luxurious strands of her hair.

She wrapped her legs around his torso and pulled him deeper inside of her.

He whispered her name on ragged breaths, like a chant of love. He kissed her lips, her breasts.

Long moments later, as their bodies moved together—passion giving, passion taking, spirits touching, hearts racing—ecstasy seized them, and both wished it would never let go.

Jake lay beside her on the bed, one arm draped casually over his eyes.

The room was steeped in inky shadows, only the pale, waning rays of a sun that had already slipped beyond the distant hills penetrating the near-total darkness.

Clanci propped her elbow on a pillow and her head against a closed fist and looked at Jake. She watched the steady rise and fall of his chest. Desire began to stir deep within her, shocking her with the realization that she wanted him to make love to her again, right then.

He moved his arm, dropping it to the pillow above his head, and his gaze met hers, strong and steady, asking questions his lips had yet to murmur.

She smiled.

He reached up and lightly caressed her cheek with the back of his hand, then slipped it around her shoulders and pulled her down to him.

Twenty minutes later the ringing of the phone startled her awake.

TWELVE

Clanci's eyes fluttered open and she stirred lazily as the ringing echo of the phone penetrated her sleep. She lay still, momentarily confused at the hard, hot surface of her pillow. Then she bolted upright and stared down at Jake. What had she done?

The phone rang again.

She scrambled from the bed, snatching her robe off a chair as she passed, and grabbed the phone in the kitchen. "Hello?"

"Clanci, I got him," Harlen said, excitement lacing his voice. "Well, I mean, I don't have him just yet, but I'm close. I've seen him, and I got a plan. But I'll be another hour or so, honey, so just sit tight. Put on a pot of coffee, would ya? And maybe fry me up a steak and some potatoes. Damned cold out here, and I'm about as hungry as a coyote on a glacier. Rotten low-life Walkers. More trouble than a bag of—"

"Grandpa, where are you?" she wailed softly, cutting him off while struggling to get the robe on.

"Over by the Pe—crap! I don't know what in tarnation's going on, but they're moving him again. Gotta go before I lose 'em."

"Grandpa!"

She looked at the handset, considered slamming it down, and settled it back on its hook with a deliberate and quiet snap instead. He kept hanging up on her, and that was becoming frustrating as all get-out. She glanced toward the open bedroom door. What would her grandfather say if he knew she'd just made love to Jake Walker?

"Probably nothing good," she mumbled to herself.

Fluffles jumped from the back of the couch and pranced to the door, looking over her shoulder and meowing. "Okay, okay," Clanci said, and walked to the door. The minute she flicked on the porch light and opened the door for the cat, she saw Buster's head pop into sight in the cab of Jake's truck.

"Oh no." She clutched the robe around her and walked to the edge of the porch. "Buster, come here," she called softly.

The dog merely looked at her.

"Buster!"

He lay back down.

Clanci cursed softly. He had obviously decided to take advantage of the fact that she'd left the driver's window of Jake's truck open. She could only hope he hadn't pranced through the goldfish pond behind the cottage before he'd jumped into the truck. Then an even worse thought struck her. Sometimes, on warm summer nights, Buster not only liked to prance through the pond, but he also liked to lie down in it. She tiptoed back to the bedroom door and glanced in quickly, crossing her fingers as she did. Relief instantly washed over her. Jake was still asleep. Clanci hurried back to the front door and stepped out onto the porch. Sliding her feet into a pair of old rubber galoshes she left there for use around the place when it rained, she held up the end of her long robe and moved toward the steps.

King Henry appeared on the porch, seemingly out of nowhere, and ran past her.

"No," Clanci screamed, but it was too late.

He bounded across the yard.

Visions of a plump tom roasting in her oven ran through her head. She tried to run toward the truck. One rubber boot slipped from her foot and folded beneath her. Clanci tripped. With arms flailing and a few choice curses rolling off her tongue, she stumbled forward, fighting to regain her balance. She nearly crashed into the side of Jake's truck. Shock yielded almost instantly to anger. "Make a note," she grumbled to herself, straightening. "Call Foster Farms in the morning and find out how much they'll give for a nasty, twenty-pound rooster." She jerked the truck door open and found her worst fears confirmed. Mud was all over the seat. She tore her gaze from the smeary mess and glared at the dog. "Buster, get out here," she ordered sternly.

The dog, sprawled on the front seat, looked at her warily and inched away.

"Buster, out!" Clanci snapped. "Now."

He scrambled toward her, sending several sheets of paper, cards, and envelopes she hadn't noticed lying on the seat flying through the air and onto the floor.

"Oh, rats." Clanci groaned.

Buster accidentally knocked against her as he leaped out of the truck, and Clanci was thrown back against the door. She counted to ten in an attempt to cool her mounting temper. It only half worked. She leaned across the seat and gathered up the papers, then slammed them into a pile in the center of the seat. Unlike the others, the top one was colorful and caught her eye. Picking it up, she realized it was a brochure and held it up toward the overhead light to get a better view.

WALKER ACRES was printed in a blaze of red across the front, with a full-color picture of a mountain scene below. More than curious, Clanci opened the brochure. Several pictures of Jake's ranch were displayed inside, including the main house and a long list of the activities and amenities a guest could expect to enjoy during a stay there.

Clanci's gaze moved quickly over the list, and she was just about to close the brochure and toss it back onto the seat when her eye was caught by the last two items: boat rentals and jet skiing.

Unbridled fury exploded within her like a volcanic blast. "I should have known!" she muttered,

her tone full of self-loathing. Crumpling the brochure in her fist, she spun around and marched back
to the cottage.

Buster barely made it into the house on her heels
before she slammed the door with a reverberating
thud.

Jake bolted upright in the bed, momentarily disoriented and wondering if a shotgun had just blasted
next to his ear.

King Henry stood next to the refrigerator, once
again pecking at Fluffles's bowl of dry cat food.

Buster took one look at the huge bird and
headed for his spot under the dining table.

Clanci ignored both of them and tromped
toward the bedroom. The toe of one of her galoshes
hooked onto the shag rug lying across the doorway
and she tripped.

Jake propped himself up on one elbow and
smiled as his gaze raked over her. "Well, that's an
interesting getup."

She stalked across the room and stopped beside
the bed to glare down at him. "How could you?"
she said. "I've seen some pretty dirty, rotten, low-
down things in my time, but you take the royal cake,
Jake Walker! You are really the lowest of the low."

"Wh-what?" Jake stared up at her, then looked
around the room quickly.

"What?" she mimicked, screwing up her face at
him. "That's good, Jake. Pretend confusion. But I
expected better. And to think I was stupid enough to
start believing you. Hah!" She threw the brochure

at him, stalked to the window, then turned back to face him.

His gaze quickly took in the fact that, with the sunlight streaming through the window at her back, he could see right through her thin robe. He looked at the dirty galoshes on her feet, then back up at the wild mane of her hair. If it wasn't so obvious she was furious with him, he would have laughed.

"How could you be so . . . so . . ." She slammed a fist onto the windowsill, unable to even think of a word to describe what she thought of him.

Jake picked up the brochure and stared at it, then looked back up at her. "What?" he said again, totally puzzled.

She picked his jeans up off the floor and threw them at him. "Oh! You are impossible. The absolute worst. What were you trying to do, Jake, seduce me into seeing things your way? Make me so crazy about you that I'd do whatever you wanted? Like maybe sign those papers that creepy salesman of yours keeps bringing here? Or did you bring them yourself?" She picked up his shirt and rifled through the pockets, then threw the garment at him.

He slapped both the pants and shirt aside and bounded, buck-naked, from the bed.

Clanci gasped and stepped back, but it was too late. Jake grabbed her by the arms and dragged her up against him.

"Let me go, you rat!" she spat out, trying to twist away from him.

"What the hell is going on?" he demanded, his

fingers tightening against her struggles. "What's the matter with you?"

She stilled and looked up at him, cold fury flashing in her eyes. "You lied."

His dark brows slanted in thought. "About what?"

"Oh! You are so thoroughly despicable," Clanci hissed. Twisting away from him, she dashed into the living room, and as one of the dirty galoshes flew off her foot, she lunged for her shotgun.

Jake grabbed the barrel as she swung it around toward him. He pushed it to one side. What the hell had she intended to do? Kill him? He jerked the weapon out of her hands. "What the blazes is the matter with you?" he thundered.

Buster, who'd come out from under the table as Clanci dashed through the room, crouched nearby, hackles raised, and growled softly, his eyes riveted on Jake.

"Get him!" Clanci yelled.

"Stay!" Jake bellowed, pointing at the dog.

Buster looked from one to the other, but didn't move.

Clanci moaned to herself. Why hadn't she ever taught Buster to attack? Reaching toward an end table, she grabbed a small vase of flowers and threw them at Jake.

He caught the vase but not the flowers. They flew over his shoulder as cold water splashed down the front of his body. He jerked in response.

"Geez," he cursed, shuddering. "What the hell is the matter with you?"

Pushing past him, she stalked into the bedroom and snatched the brochure off the bed. Turning and seeing he was right on her heels, she thrust it at his chest. "This is what's the matter with me!"

He looked at the brochure. "I don't . . ."

"You don't . . . you don't," she mocked. "Well, what I don't is know how I could have been so stupid as to believe anything you said," Clanci snapped, pushing past him again and walking to the window. She spun around. "Especially that," she said, pointing at the bed. "Where's Blue? What have you done with him? And my grandfather. What do you have, Jake, men out there leading my grandfather on some wild-goose chase?" She began to pace. "He's old, Jake. Nearly eighty-one. He could get pneumonia. Have a heart attack or a stroke." She stopped and glowered at him. "I should have let you try to drive yourself into a damned tree."

"You're the one who drugged me and drove me here, remember?" he said.

"Maybe you weren't really out of it at all," Clanci countered. "Maybe you knew what I was trying to do and had a plan of your own all set up. Like maybe the beer I put the potion in wasn't even the one you drank."

Jake shook his head. "And maybe you're just plain crazy, Clanci."

She looked at him, her gaze moving over his naked body. She suddenly felt sick at what she'd done.

"Oh, Lord." She moaned beneath her breath and leaned back against the windowsill. She'd gone to bed with Jake Walker. She should have known better. Hadn't her grandfather warned her about him? Hadn't her disaster with Alex taught her anything? Given her any insight into men? Into herself? She didn't know whom she hated more at the moment: Jake or herself. "Just get your clothes on and get out of my house."

Tossing the shotgun to the bed, Jake crossed the room and grabbed her by the arms again. "Not until you tell me what the hell is wrong." He thrust the brochure under her nose. "What's this all about?"

She glared at him through narrowed eyes. "You said you didn't sabotage the Lazy J."

"That's right, I didn't."

"You said you didn't steal Blue."

"I didn't."

She snatched the brochure from his hand. "Your little dude ranch can't offer jet skiing, Jake," Clanci said, "or any other kind of river sport unless you have unrestricted access to the river that runs through the Lazy J, and that's something you don't have."

The frown that cut into his brow, and the troubled look that darkened his eyes, gave her a start. He took the brochure from her and, walking to the bureau, smoothed out the wrinkled paper and stared down at it. His gaze moved over the type. A moment later he turned back to face her. "I didn't know about this," he said softly.

She scoffed. "Oh, yeah, right. I'm supposed to believe that? It was in your truck, Jake. It's your ranch. It's your brochure."

He shook his head as a sick feeling took root in the pit of his stomach. The suspicions he'd been fighting since the first moment Clanci had mentioned the sabotaging incidents and the theft of her horse now loomed over him like a dark cloud he couldn't ignore. He'd tried to rationalize them away, tried to tell himself there had to be another answer, but in the back of his mind he'd always known. His fingers clenched into a fist, dragging the brochure with them and turning it into a small, unrecognizable wad. He had seen brochures on his sister's desk, but since she was running her part of the ranch as a dude ranch, he'd never paid any attention to them. Why should he? They hadn't had anything to do with his business. That had been his mistake.

Jake cursed softly. He even remembered the night she'd come into his office and asked him to look at the new brochure. He'd been busy going over his books and hadn't paid much attention, mumbling that he'd do it later. She must have tucked it into his papers. He shook his head and looked at Clanci. "I didn't know," he said.

"Right," Clanci said with a sneer. "Things happen on your ranch and you don't know about them."

He grabbed his jeans and climbed into them. "Evidently that's about it, but not anymore."

"Drop the act, Jake," Clanci said, "you'd never make it in Hollywood."

He tugged on his shirt, slipped on his boots, and closed the distance between them, dragging her twisting and writhing into his arms. "Would you just stop spitting venom and listen to me for a minute?"

"Listen to more of your lies, Jake?" She shook her head violently and pushed against him. "I don't think so."

She was the most stubborn woman he'd ever met. And he had to be totally insane, because if he wasn't so damned angry at the moment, and didn't have to get back to his own ranch, he'd like nothing better than to rip her robe off and make love to her until the sun came back up. "I'll make this right, Clanci," he said softly, pausing to stare deeply into her eyes. "I told you, I don't want your ranch, or your river."

She stared up at him, the flames of outrage dancing in her eyes. *I only want you.* The words he'd spoken earlier whispered through her memory. She slapped at the hand in which he still held the brochure. "Well, you certainly have a funny way of showing that."

Without thought or reason, Jake dragged Clanci into his arms and buried her lips beneath his in a savage kiss, one born of desperation and need.

She slapped at his shoulders, even as she felt the fireworks of desire exploding within her. She couldn't give in to him. She couldn't. But she couldn't resist him either.

With his strong hands circling her upper arms, Jake pulled away from her and held her in front of him. "Get yourself together," he ordered, his own eyes blazing with fury. "We're going to find your grandfather and find out just what the blazes is going on around here."

"Hmmph! Like you don't know."

He ignored the snipe. "I'll wait in the truck."

Clanci remembered the mud Buster had left all over Jake's front seat. She opened her mouth to warn him, then snapped it shut. What did she care? Let him sit in it. Maybe, if she was lucky, it would come alive and attack him.

When Jake jerked the door of his truck open, the overhead light went on. His jaw dropped. He stared in disbelief. "What the . . . ?"

Henry scooted around him and jumped into the cab, perching on the back of the seat and looking about arrogantly.

Jake climbed halfway into the truck, grabbed a newspaper from the backseat, and scrubbed it over the front, wiping away the mud. He'd no sooner finished doing this and was about to climb in behind the wheel than Buster bounded past him, jumped onto the seat, and skidded across it to the other side.

Henry squawked loudly and dived for the backseat.

Jake stared at the dog. "Get off there," he ordered, and pointed to the floor.

Buster threw him a soulful look and slunk to the floor on the passenger side of the cab.

Clanci held the phone in her hand, and watching through the window to make certain Jake was at his truck and out of earshot, she dialed her grandfather's cell-phone number, praying he wasn't someplace where it would be heard and land him in trouble.

"I'm sorry," a recording of the operator said, "but the number you're calling is temporarily out of range or service."

Clanci felt her world threaten to stop spinning. She slammed the phone down and ran for the front door. At Jake's truck she swung the passenger door open and started to climb in. Her toe hit Buster's rump and, thrown off balance, she landed facedown on the seat, sputtering and cursing.

Jake tried not to laugh but wasn't totally successful.

Clanci pushed herself up, threw him a look that was meant to kill, tossed another to Buster, and settled herself on the seat. Maybe she should have called the sheriff. She glanced back at the cottage. Too late now. But she wasn't going to tell Jake about her grandfather's phone. If they did run into trouble out there, she might have to fake using it to call the sheriff to keep Jake or his men from doing something drastic. "Let's get this charade over with," she said. "And if you or your sister have hurt my grandfather, I'll sue you for everything you're worth."

Jake climbed into the truck, slammed the door, and started the engine. It roared to life and all but shattered the silence of the night. He had to be nuts to put stock in anything Clanci James said. For all he knew, her grandfather was off on vacation, or a mindless tangent, and her precious horse could be anywhere, including her own pasture. After all, Barbara was his sister. Why would she jeopardize everything with some harebrained scheme? They had access to the river for his cattle, and that's all they really needed.

He glanced at Clanci as he peeled away from the house. She might be one of the sexiest woman he'd ever had the pleasure of sharing a bed with, but he was beginning to wonder if she was also certifiably crazy. Trying to convince himself of that was preferable to the suspicion that Barbara had actually engineered a scheme to drive the Jameses off their property.

In the distance a coyote howled.

Buster started to answer.

"Shut up," Jake snapped.

Buster slunk back to the floor, looking for all the world like his best friend had just scolded him.

"He was just doing what comes natural," Clanci said.

"So am I," Jake growled. He shoved the gearshift into place and spun away from the road. Going across their properties would be quicker.

His hands held tight to the wheel, his knuckles nearly white. It had been a long time since he'd been so angry, and he didn't like the feeling. He'd thought life on the ranch would be easygoing, smooth, calm, and quiet. He should have known better. His life had never been easygoing, smooth, calm, or quiet, and it looked to be a pretty good bet that it never would be.

Halfway down the drive Jake slammed on the brakes and skidded to a stop. "This isn't going to work. If your grandfather is anywhere around here and sees us approaching in this truck, he'll take off."

Clanci started to make a sneering remark but stopped. If Jake's people weren't holding her grandfather someplace and he was out looking for Blue, then Jake was right. The minute Harlen saw the lights of a vehicle approaching, he'd hide, and when he recognized it as Jake's truck, he'd make certain they didn't find him, even if he saw Clanci with Jake. He'd just figure it was a trick. That they'd kidnapped her too.

She stared at him, wondering again if they were wrong about him . . . wanting to have been wrong about him, and knowing she couldn't take the chance of letting her guard down. No matter how much she wanted to. Not yet.

Jake jammed the gearshift into reverse and floored the accelerator. The truck sped backward, coming to a stop in front of the barn. Throwing his door open, he climbed out and stalked inside the moonlit structure.

Clanci, trying to figure out what he was doing, scrambled out and ran after him.

He grabbed two saddles from a rack near the door. "Which ones?" he asked, turning to stare at the stalled horses.

Her gaze darted from him to the two saddles he was holding.

"We have a better chance of finding your grandfather if he doesn't see two headlights bouncing over the hills toward him."

Clanci nodded. "Kelly and Boz," she said, pointing to the two rear paddocks. She threw open their gates and the geldings pranced into the center of the barn.

Jake hurriedly saddled one while Clanci did the other.

She swung up onto Boz's back as Jake mounted Kelly, then bent to readjust one of his stirrups.

Grabbing one of the saddlebags her grandfather always kept packed with survival supplies, Clanci urged Boz out of the barn and into the night.

"Did Harlen give you any idea of his location when he called?" Jake asked, maneuvering Kelly up beside her. "I've got two thousand acres over there."

His mouth was tight and grim. In spite of herself, Clanci remembered how good it had felt pressed to hers. Suddenly thoughts of Rick and Alex invaded her mind and she wondered if all the good-looking ones were scoundrels, or if it was just her luck to be drawn to that sort.

"Clanci? We need a starting point."

Her thoughts jerked back to reality. "He didn't say where he was. All he said was that he'd seen Blue and would be home in about two hours." Why was she helping him?

"He must have said something more," Jake urged. "Anything?"

She looked at him, still not willing to trust.

"Clanci, dammit," Jake exploded. "I'm trying to help you. Harlen might be hurt out there somewhere, or . . ."

"Or?" she repeated, brows rising.

"Or nothing," he grumbled, not willing to say the word *dead* and risk her going into hysterics.

"Jail?" Clanci snapped. "Or locked up in your barn?"

"If he was in jail, I'm sure you would have heard, and I doubt he'd go unnoticed in my barn. The place is a dude ranch, remember?"

Her eyes narrowed, and she stared down at the ground without actually seeing it as another thought nagged at her. She remembered the gun nestled in the saddlebag she'd grabbed and figured she would trust Jake, but only sparingly. "That's all he said except . . ."

"Except what?"

"Well, he started to say P . . . or Pay . . . or something like that, but he didn't finish it."

"Pay?" Jake echoed, looking thoughtfully into the distance. "Pay?" He jerked around in his saddle and looked at her. "Like Pele maybe? As in Pele's Peak?"

Her eyes widened slightly.

"Last time he called," Jake went on, "he said he'd be here in two hours, right?"

She nodded.

"So give him half an hour to get the horse, and another hour and a half to get back to the Lazy J and the house. That means he had to be a good distance off. Probably on the other side of Walker Acres from your boundary." His eyes narrowed as he calculated things out. Finally he nodded, as if satisfied with the direction of his thoughts. "Pele's Peak is at one end of Wildcat Canyon. That would be about the right distance."

Clanci hoped not. Pele's Peak might have been sacred ground to the ancient Indians, but Wildcat Canyon was something quite different. In the dark, the canyon wasn't exactly the safest terrain to travel. Its plateaus dropped sharply, its canyon walls were sheer vertical drops in most places, and ancient glacier pits and holes dotted the landscape while jagged rocks pierced it in others. The Indians had never liked Wildcat Canyon, referring to it as a place where evil spirits dwelled, waiting to attack a man and claim his soul.

"Maybe we should split up," Jake suggested an hour later. They'd come across no sign of Harlen, and he was beginning to believe they weren't going to. "You go north. I'll try going south."

Clanci looked at him, not bothering to mask the suspicion she knew was on her face. "Why? Are we getting too close to where you stashed Blue?"

Without a word, Jake jerked his horse's reins and the animal wheeled around and took off in a lope.

Startled, Clanci watched for a few seconds, then nudged Boz into a full gallop in the same direction. They easily caught up to Jake and Kelly a few minutes later. "We stay together," she shouted.

"Fine," Jake snapped, not even bothering to look at her.

They rode for another hour before Jake reined in again. He leaned an arm on his saddle horn and looked at Clanci. "This isn't getting us anywhere. We're riding around in the dark, taking a chance on killing ourselves, and we could have ridden within a few yards of Harlen and not known it. Why don't you ride back to your house?" he suggested. "I'll go to mine and see if I can find out anything there."

"That would give you plenty of time to move Blue, wouldn't it?"

"Woman, you really are the—" Jake sighed. He was getting real tired of being called a thief by a woman he'd just made love to and had thought, in spite of the way the evening had begun, that maybe, just maybe they'd . . . He banished the thought. It was ridiculous anyway. His experience with Katherine had taught him that trust was one of the most important things in a relationship, and there certainly wasn't any of that between him and Clanci. In fact, they were working at a definite minus in that department. "You still don't believe I'm trying to help you, do you?" he challenged.

"I want to," Clanci said truthfully.

"But you don't." He turned away from her and stared at the mountains in the distance, a ragged silhouette of blackness against a slightly paler sky. He'd heard the rumors in town; the Jameses had experienced a streak of bad luck, Harlen had mortgaged the house after the death of his son. Obviously, they'd been counting on the money from studding out Blue to help get them caught up with things. If the situation was reversed, he probably wouldn't believe her either, but that didn't make this whole mess any easier to swallow, especially the fact that he was pretty certain his sister was behind it all. He looked back at Clanci. "Maybe I can't blame you for not trusting me. Fine. But riding around out here all night obviously isn't getting us anywhere. I'm going to my place. You can come with me if you want, or you can go home. I just thought maybe Harlen might have returned to your place by now. Or called." He turned his horse. "But it's your choice."

Clanci watched him ride away, torn as to what to do. What he'd suggested made sense—*if* she believed that he hadn't had anything to do with stealing Blue or sabotaging the Lazy J. And that his men hadn't already nabbed her grandfather and carted him off somewhere. She closed her eyes. It was what she desperately wanted to believe.

He could have walked out on her the moment he'd gotten himself free. He could have called the sheriff and charged her with kidnapping, or at the very least, with assault. He could have gone straight back to his ranch and hunted down her grandfather. Instead, he'd stayed with her, gone out of his way to make her feel comfortable with him . . . to make her feel she could trust him.

Her experience with her ex-husband had come close to souring her on trusting any man other than her grandfather. She opened her eyes to watch Jake's retreating figure disappear into the darkness. She suddenly knew how much she wanted to trust him.

But if she was wrong . . . she bit down on her lower lip and turned to look over her shoulder toward the Lazy J, then back at Jake. She stood in her stirrups. "Call me in an hour," she called out.

"Fine," he threw over his shoulder, not even bothering to turn and look back at her.

THIRTEEN

The morning sun was just starting to peek over the far-off hills and bathe the valley in a warm haze when Jake reined in atop a small knoll overlooking the main buildings of Walker Acres.

His whole world was tilting on its axis and threatening to spin out of control, and all because of a spitfire who was almost too stubborn and too impulsive for her own good.

And made him feel things that he wanted to feel forever.

He stared down at the long low ranch house. It had been more to his liking when he'd first purchased the place. Then it had been a simple, sixty-year-old wooden ranch house surrounded by various outbuildings and corrals. But Barbara had done a lot of remodeling and adding on in the past nine months, banishing the structure's original country-style simplicity and turning it into a large Spanish hacienda, complete with arches, French doors, covered terraces, a tiled roof, and bougainvillea-draped trellises. She'd also had a swimming pool and hot tub installed in the backyard, a sprawling brick patio with built-in barbeque, and both badminton and tennis courts.

Jake sighed and pressed his heels to Kelly's ribs. The horse instantly moved forward and down the hill.

He'd lost his heart to Clanci and ended up suspecting his sister of being a thief, all in a matter of hours. He felt good inside, and he felt like hell.

An image of Clanci's face filled Jake's mind, along with the memory of making love to her. She was everything he'd thought he didn't want in a woman, and everything, he knew now, he desperately wanted and needed.

In front of the barn one of his wranglers was repairing a horse's shoe. He paused as Jake rode up, then dropped the horse's leg and moved away from the animal.

"Hey, boss." The man grinned crookedly and, pulling a kerchief from his back pocket, wiped it across the back of his neck, then peered up at Jake from beneath an oversized cowboy hat. "What'd you do, leave your truck up in Dallas and get home the old-fashioned way?"

Jake ignored the gibe and dismounted. "Rub the horse down, would you, Hank?" He turned toward the house, then stopped. "Where's Barbara?"

"Took a group of slicks out on a ride about half

an hour ago. Said they were gonna watch the sun come up." He shook his head, as if in wonder. "Never have figured out why anybody'd get up just to do that." He grabbed Kelly's reins and turned toward the barn.

Jake followed him inside. "You haven't seen an old man poking around out here anywhere, have you, Hank?"

The young wrangler looked at Jake, his freckle-covered, boyish face breaking into a smug smile. "Hell, Jake, most of the slicks that come here seem at least a half century or better. How old you talking, anyway?"

"Harlen James," Jake said. "The old man who owns the spread that borders our west pasture."

Hank shook his head, sending long red curls spreading across his shoulders. "Nah. I've seen him around town, at the supply store and such, but can't say I've seen him here. He supposed to be visiting or something?"

"Or something," Jake grumbled. He didn't even want to think about how Clanci would take it if anything had happened to her grandfather.

"Well, only person I've seen around here I didn't know was that new guy."

Jake's attention was caught. "What new guy?"

Hank shrugged. "Don't know his name. I seen someone drive away from the barn this morning just before your sister and her group left. He was hauling one of our horse trailers behind his rig, and I didn't recognize him. I figured with it being dark, and you gone off to Dallas and all, I'd better look into it, make sure there wasn't anything funny going on. You know, like a thief or something?"

Jake nodded.

"Well, I went up to the house and I mentioned what I'd seen to your sister, and she said it was just the new guy she'd hired, and I didn't need to concern myself about it."

"And he took one of our horse trailers?"

Hank nodded. "Yeah. Barbara said she'd sent him into town with a horse she'd sold."

Jake didn't like the way the conversation was going, but he had to admit it wasn't exactly a surprise. "What horse?" he asked Hank. "Which horse is she selling?"

Hank shrugged again. "Beats the tar outta me, Jake. She didn't say, and truth be told, I ain't noticed none of them gone."

Jake did a quick inventory of the horses stabled in the barn.

None was missing.

"How many slicks went out with my sister this morning?" he asked Hank.

The young man stopped brushing Kelly and looked up. "Six, I think. Four women and two men."

Without another word to Hank, Jake walked to the corrals where some of the horses his sister used for trail rides were waiting to be shoed. Minutes later he climbed into one of the ranch Jeeps. Leaving a cloud of dust behind him as he peeled away from the barn, he drove to the grazing pastures. It took him over an hour to make the count. "Dammit, why?" he barked aloud, and slammed a fist against the steering wheel. A sense of hurt and anger raged through him, twisting his gut into knots and inciting a deep throbbing at his temples.

As far as he could tell, there were no horses missing except the ones Barbara had taken on her ride. All the brood mares, foals, and geldings were accounted for.

Jake slunk down in the Jeep's seat and a half-dozen curses spilled from his lips. He hadn't wanted to be right, but he didn't see now how he could be wrong.

Clanci paced the small living room of her cottage, then stopped and looked across the room at the clock on the wall. Jake should have called over forty-five minutes ago. She reached for the phone and started to dial the number for the sheriff's office, then slammed the handset back down onto its cradle. How could she call Rick Murdock? What would she tell him? Her grandfather was convinced Jake Walker stole Blue, so he went to steal him back, and while she waited for him to return she went to Sam's Bar & Grill and drugged Jake so he couldn't go home and catch her grandfather. But she'd given him too much of her grandfather's quieting potion and nearly knocked him out, so she'd brought him home to her place and just happened to end up making love to him . . . and worse, falling in love with him, and oh, by the way, the reason she was calling now was because they were all missing—Jake, Blue, and her grandfather.

Oh, Rick would really help her after hearing that story, she thought wryly. She struggled against the tears that had been wanting to burst from her eyes for the last hour, and tried to ignore the fact that her stomach felt as if its bottom had dropped out.

She walked to the window for the umpteenth time since she'd gotten home and slapped the curtain back. There was no sign of her grandfather or Jake.

Buster lumbered to the door and threw her a beseeching look to be let out. Clanci opened the door and shrieked as King Henry ran past her and into the cottage.

"Blast you, bird!" she screamed.

Fluffles, who'd been curled in a ball on the couch and sleeping peacefully, instantly shot to her feet, back arched, eyes wide, and hair standing on end. She hissed loudly, baring her fangs.

Henry charged.

Clanci screamed again, and Fluffles turned and frantically scratched her way up the drapes.

Henry puffed his chest out, as if proud of himself, then turned and walked arrogantly into Clanci's bedroom. She slammed the door, marched into her bedroom, and looked around for the rooster. He was nowhere in sight. Great. Now she had Henry the rooster Houdini in her bedroom. She bent down. "Here, Henry," she called softly. "Come on out, Henry. Pssst-pssst. Henry?" She finally found him under the bed. "Come out of there or you'll be dinner," she said, glaring at him while crouching down on hands and knees.

The bird didn't budge.

Obviously, threatening to cook him wasn't a great incentive for cooperation.

Clanci sat down, settling her back against her nightstand. Suddenly she felt like just giving in to the tears that had been plaguing the back of her eyes for hours. How could such a simple plan have gotten so thoroughly messed up? Harlen was supposed to locate Blue, take some pictures—which would hopefully include incriminating evidence against the Walkers—then get the horse and come home. All she was supposed to have done was detain Jake at the bar for a few hours. That was it. A simple plan— a couple of hours' effort.

A pounding on her front door startled Clanci out of her bout of self-pity. Jumping to her feet, she ran to the door and flung it open. "Jake," she said breathlessly.

His eyes raked over her. The urge to drag her into his arms gripped him, but he shrugged it aside. His body might be in the mood for that kind of thing, but he wasn't. His mood was about as black as it had ever been, but he had a feeling it was going to get worse. "Get your shoes on," he ordered, noticing she was in her stocking feet. "We've got to go."

Henry, obviously hearing Jake's voice, ran from

the bedroom, squawking loudly in welcome, or maybe protest at having been left behind.

"Get in the truck, Henry," Jake said.

Clanci grabbed her boots. "Where are we going?"

Sharing his suspicions, which he had no doubt were now going to turn into some nasty facts, was the last thing he wanted to do at the moment. "Town," he growled grudgingly.

Clanci hopped on one foot while struggling to pull on her other boot. She started to lose her balance and grabbed for Jake.

His arms reached out for her instinctively.

She fell against his chest.

The heady scent of Clanci and jasmine instantly filled his senses, while the feel of her in his arms stoked the sleeping desires he was trying to keep in check.

"Clanci, dammit," Jake said, setting her away from him, "we don't have time for that now. Let's just go."

Startled, and a bit put off, Clanci stiffened. "I wasn't making a pass at you, Jake Walker," she snapped. "I merely lost my balance."

He felt instantly contrite, knowing he'd taken his bad temper out on her needlessly. "Fine. Sorry," he mumbled. "Are you ready?"

"To do what?" she demanded, her tone dripping icicles as she stared at him, hands clenched and rammed onto her hips.

"Barbara hired a new wrangler while I was supposed to be in Dallas yesterday," he practically spit out, glaring back at her, "and according to one of my men, the guy took off for town this morning to sell one of Barbara's horses."

Clanci frowned. "So?"

"So, as far as I can tell," Jake said, "all of our horses are accounted for. That's why I'm late getting back to you."

"You mean . . . ?"

"Yeah, I think so," Jake said, hoping he was wrong.

FOURTEEN

"Murdock's favorite speed trap is right up here," Clanci said as they neared the last curve in the road leading into Coyote Bend.

"Yeah, I know, he's already caught me twice on it." Jake shifted the truck into third gear.

Moments later, as they were about to pass EmmyLou's Diner, he slammed on the brakes.

Clanci flew forward.

The truck's tires squealed and the vehicle fishtailed.

Clanci's seat belt locked, and she was yanked violently back against her seat. The breath in her lungs flew out, and her stomach disappeared.

"What the heck was that for?" she demanded, jerking around to face him the moment the truck stopped and she regained some breath.

"Look." He nodded toward the diner's parking lot.

She looked in the direction he indicated and saw a pickup and horse trailer parked in the side lot. On the side of the white trailer, painted in large, red letters, was WALKER ACRES.

Jake rammed the gearshift into reverse and slammed his foot down on the accelerator.

Clanci was thrown forward as she frantically reached out for the door's grab handle.

King Henry tumbled from the back of the front seat, squawking loudly.

Clanci shrieked and slapped at the bird's wing as Henry flapped them wildly, repeatedly smacking her in the head.

"Henry, dammit," Jake thundered, slamming on his brakes again and pushing the bird's other wing away from his face and the steering wheel. He rammed his foot down on the accelerator and the truck again sped backward. Jake jerked on the steering wheel, the truck spun around, tilting precariously as it did, then shot forward into a parking place in front of the diner.

Clanci, still tightly gripping the grab handle, sagged against the door as the truck stopped, certain both her heart and her stomach were back on the road somewhere.

Jake threw open his door. "Come on."

She turned to see him stalking toward the trailer. Clanci scrambled from the truck and nearly sagged to the ground on legs that suddenly resembled melting rubber. Only her grip on the door's handle kept her from meeting the ground face-first. Inhaling deeply and shaking herself, she regained at least enough composure to remain upright, and ran after him.

Jake stopped abruptly beside the trailer.

Clanci plowed into his back.

Jake's face smashed into the side of the trailer, and he let loose with a loud but garbled curse of startled pain.

She pushed herself away immediately. "Sorry," she mumbled. "Are you hurt?"

"No, I always wanted a flat face anyway."

"Sorry," she mumbled again.

He rubbed at his nose and looked down at her. "You can make up for it later."

She saw the gleam of devilry in his eyes and felt a warm flush instantly sweep through her body.

Jake glanced back at the trailer. "It's empty."

"So, now what?" she asked, her hands trembling slightly as part of her mind strayed from the business at hand and thought about his "later."

Without another word he turned and stomped toward the diner's entrance.

She ran after him. "What are you going to do?"

Two feet inside he stopped and looked around. "Who's driving the Walker Acres rig parked outside?" he demanded loudly.

Several people turned and glanced at him. Other than a middle-aged couple who looked like tourists, a trucker, and one or two wranglers, Clanci recognized everyone in the place.

"I am," one of the wranglers called out. He

waved a gnarled hand at Jake and squinted at him from beneath a cowboy hat that had seen better days. "Why? The rig blocking something?"

Clanci followed Jake as he walked over to the man's booth and, leaning forward, stuck his face into the other man's. "It's my rig, mister, and I'd kinda like to know what you're doing with it."

The man instantly straightened in his seat, his face turning a little paler beneath the deep tan covering his leatherlike skin. "I was hired yesterday by Barbara Walker and told to transport a horse to town this morning. You saying that rig was stolen, or something?"

"So where's the horse?" Jake asked, not answering the man and moving an inch.

"Transferred over to his new owner."

Clanci felt her heart nearly stop.

Jake's shoulders flinched as his right hand curled into a fist, and he slammed it violently down on the table. "What new owner?" he thundered, his voice filling the entire restaurant.

Every eye in the place was on him, including Clanci's.

The man squirmed in his seat, pushing back as if trying to put a little more distance between himself and the madman who was hovering over him. "I don't know the guy's name. I was just told to bring the horse here, that's all. Guy met me, handed over a receipt for sale, and took the horse. Loaded it into one of those semihaulers."

"Semihauler?" Jake echoed, not at all liking where he figured this conversation was headed.

"Yeah. From the slaughterhouse over in Kimball."

Clanci's knees nearly buckled beneath her. Blue was on his way to a slaughterhouse. She grabbed for the back of the nearest booth and clutched it tightly, calling on all her strength to remain upright.

Jake wheeled around and grabbed Clanci's hand, dragging her up against him then slipping his arm around her waist and holding her tight. He glared back down at the man. "How long ago?" he demanded.

The man glanced at the clock over the counter. "Thirty, maybe forty minutes."

Setting Clanci away from him hurriedly, he grabbed her hand and ran out of the diner, half hauling, half dragging her behind him. "Come on," he ordered as they neared the truck. He threw open her door and, not waiting to help her in, ran around to the driver's side.

Moments later they sped through town, the streets nearly deserted because of the early hour.

The sheriff's office came into sight.

Clanci closed her eyes and prayed Rick Murdock and his deputy were out playing detective somewhere, or trying to catch unsuspecting truckers coming a little too fast over the grade into town.

Ten miles and a few minutes later they saw what appeared to be a stock truck pulled over to the side of the road in the distance.

"Look," Clanci said, pointing at the truck as they drew nearer. "I think that's my grandfather's horse by that truck."

"And that looks like your grandfather," Jake snapped, nodding toward two men dancing about the side of the road between the semi and the horse and dodging each other's fists.

"Oh no."

Jake slammed on the brakes, and the moment the truck stopped, Clanci threw open her door and jumped out, running toward the men. "Grandpa, stop!" she yelled. "Stop."

Jake barged between the men, arms raised to deflect any blows, Henry running around at his feet.

Harlen cursed and threw a fist.

Jake caught it. "Stop," he bellowed, then accidentally stepped on Henry's foot.

The rooster screeched like someone had just sawed off his leg.

The trucker swung.

"Jake, watch out," Clanci screamed.

He moved with lightning speed to deflect the blow and caught the man's wrist.

Henry, still screeching and flapping his wings wildly, ran into the middle of the road.

The two men cursed soundly and struggled against the hold Jake had on them.

"Enough!" he bellowed. A fist struck him on the side of the jaw and he spun backward, momentarily stunned.

Henry ran at the men and began pecking indiscriminately at their legs.

Clanci grabbed at her grandfather's swinging arm, felt a huge claw scrape across her boot, and looked down just in time to see Henry's beak stab at the truck driver's calf. The man screamed and jumped away. Harlen's fist swung around and met thin air.

Jake's temper was on such a short rein now, he wasn't sure he could hold it much longer if anything else unexpected happened. He grabbed the short truck driver by the back of his shirt and hauled him farther away from Harlen, who was still cursing, struggling against Clanci's hold on him, and throwing wild punches.

"Grandpa, stop," Clanci said, for what she felt was the hundredth time in the last two minutes.

Harlen abruptly stopped swinging and, twisting away from her, glared at the truck driver. "He's got Blue in that rig," he said angrily.

"I know that, but I don't think he does," she said.

They walked to the rear of the rig, where Jake was standing with the truck driver.

"Open it," Jake ordered.

The driver's eyes widened in surprise, and Clanci thought for a moment they were going to pop out of his head. "Whaddya mean, open it? I can't do that. Them horses are bought and paid for and going to—"

"Open it," Jake demanded, "or I'll let Harlen here go at you again. And maybe this time I'll help."

The driver glanced at Harlen, then back at Jake, spat a wad of tobacco onto the ground, and with a grumbled curse, reached up and opened the padlock dangling from the gate's latch. "I unlocked it," he mumbled, "but I ain't gonna open it. Them horses git out, it's on your head, and your pocketbook. I ain't getting fired."

Jake grabbed the latch and lowered the gate.

Clanci instantly jumped up onto the lowered ramp. "There," she said, pointing to Blue, who was tethered to the wall of the hauler between two other horses.

Jake slipped between the horses and pulled Blue's rope free. "Easy, boy," he said soothingly when Blue looked around nervously and began to shuffle his feet about. "Easy. You're going home now." He backed the large stallion out of the truck and handed his lead rope to Harlen.

"Whaddaya doin' here?" Harlen spat out, snatching the rope from Jake's hand and glowering at him.

"Getting your horse back," Jack said, with a lot more calm than he felt.

"You can't just take that horse," the truck driver shrieked. "You're gonna get me fired."

"You're a thief," Harlen said, turning his reproachful glare to the truck driver.

"And you're a crazy old coot," the driver shot back. "I got a bill of sale on every horse in there."

"Liar," Harlen grumbled.

"Yeah?" The man dug into the pocket of his shirt and drew out a folded piece of paper. "Well, what do you call this, you senile old fart?"

Jake grabbed the paper and quickly looked it over.

"Riding out in front of my rig like that," the driver said, his attention still on Harlen. "Crazy codger. Nearly got us both killed."

"Would have served you right if I had," Harlen muttered.

"Shoulda just run you down," the trucker countered, spitting out a wad of tobacco.

"Enough!" Jake said with a growl.

Clanci looked at him sharply. His eyes burned with a cold rage as he glowered at the two men. He grabbed Harlen's arm and pulled him toward his pickup, then reached in for his cell phone and dialed EmmyLou's Diner.

"EmmyLou's Diner, best food west of anywhere," the waitress who answered chirped.

"Is the wrangler from Walker Acres still there?" Jake asked, sparing no words for pleasantries.

"Well, just a minute, sweetcakes, and I'll check," the waitress replied.

A moment later the man came on the line. "Yeah?"

"This is Jake Walker. Remember me?" he asked mockingly.

"Ah, yes, Mr. Walker." The edge of insolence that had been in the man's tone disappeared.

"Good. I'm on the highway, about ten miles south of the diner. I need you to bring the rig out here and pick up a horse."

"What?" the man said, obviously puzzled. "But I'm supposed to go back to the ranch and meet Miss Walker and—"

"Just do it!" Jack snapped. He clicked off the phone and threw it down on the seat, then turned back to Harlen. "One of my men is in town with a rig. I want you to wait here for him, and he'll drive you and your horses back to the Lazy J."

Harlen stared up at Jake, defiance and incredulity shining from his old eyes. "You think I'm crazy? I ain't going in no rig of yours with one of your wranglers," he said.

"Grandpa," Clanci started, walking toward them. "It's okay. Jake is—"

"Likely end up in Wildcat Canyon again," Harlen said, cutting Clanci off, "only this time I'd probably get left staked out for the buzzards."

"Grandpa! Jake's been helping me look for . . ."

He turned to Clanci. "You're in with this thieving no-good?"

Jake inhaled deeply, swore beneath his breath, and walked back to where the stock-truck driver was standing. "Whose horses have you got in there?" he asked softly.

The man shrugged. "I picked up most of them from Simpson's place over in Lallamont. That one there was the only single pickup," he said, nodding toward Blue. "Most of them are just old brood mares past their prime, and I got a couple of broken-down geldings. Why?"

"You got a bill of sale on all of them?" Jake asked, trying to ignore the grumblings of Harlen James as Clanci continued to try to make him see reason and wait for Jake's rig. He stared at the man, his gaze fringed with an icy chill.

The truck driver nodded and handed him another piece of paper, signed by Oren Simpson of Cresent Bar ranch, Lallamont, Texas.

Jake pulled out his wallet and, taking one of his business cards from it, handed it to the man. "Drive them there. Tell my foreman, Ben Gage, to put them in the south pasture and cut you a check for twenty percent over your expenses and whatever you planned on selling them for." Jake's eyes bored into the other man's. "And don't try to cheat me, or it'll be the last piece of work you ever get in this valley." He turned and started to walk away.

"You mean you wanna buy all these broken-down old nags?" the driver called after him, wide-eyed. "Why?"

Jake paused and slowly turned to look back at the man. "I don't believe in slaughterhouses," he said, anger slicing through his words.

While Harlen inspected Blue, having tired of arguing with Clanci, she had turned her attention to Jake. She watched him approach the truck. "You're really buying those horses?" she asked softly. A warm feeling was spreading all through her at the idea that he'd do such a thing.

He nodded.

"Just to save them from the slaughterhouse?"

A faint smile tugged at his lips. "I do have a few good qualities, Clanci," he said. "I don't believe any horse deserves to end up in a slaughterhouse."

She felt a sting of tears at the corners of her eyes and blinked them away. He had a lot more than a few good qualities, she thought, suddenly feeling very guilty at how drastically she'd misjudged him. He was strength and tenderness all wrapped up in one package, a man she could lean on for support, snuggle up to for comfort, and love for the rest of her life.

Jake turned to Harlen. "I didn't steal your horse, Mr. James." He glanced at Clanci as the old man took his time straightening up and turning toward him. "I didn't send anyone to make any offers to buy your ranch, and I'm not interested in gaining un-restricted access to the river. All I need is enough access for my herds, and the easement you granted me gives me that."

Harlen shoved his face toward Jake's and scrunched his features into a suspicious leer. "You think I'm fool enough to believe that?"

"It's the truth."

"Hmmph!" Harlen grunted, his eyes hard with accusation. "If it walks like a dog, smells like a dog, and sounds like a dog, then it most likely is a—"

"Grandpa," Clanci said, shocked at her grandfather's comment and attitude.

Harlen's eyes narrowed as they turned on her. "You go and let herself get sweet on this lowlife, girl?"

A burning heat swept over Clanci, scorching her cheeks, and she felt like sinking into the ground. She threw a quick glance in Jake's direction.

He was staring hard at Harlen.

Her grandfather jerked on Blue's lead rope and started walking away. "Clanci!" he yelled over his shoulder. "You come on home with me now, girl, or I swear, there ain't gonna be no home for you to be coming to."

Clanci stared after Harlen, dumbfounded. She had never seen him be so unreasonable. And never, not even once, had he threatened her that way. She looked hurriedly at Jake. "I . . ." She shook her head and shrugged. "I don't know why he's—"

"Clanci!" Harlen snapped, not even glancing back.

"I have to go, Jake."

He reached out as she turned, his hand on her arm stopping her. "Clanci . . ."

She looked into his eyes and found them suddenly hard and cold. A little stab of fear touched her heart. Was this it? She had to pick her grandfather over Jake? "I . . . I have to go. I'm sorry."

Jake watched her walk away. Why did he always pick the wrong ones?

FIFTEEN

Barbara had led the group she'd taken for a morning trail ride back into the barn area and was just dismounting when Jake pulled his truck up before the large, open doors of the barn. "Hank," Barbara said, "make sure they're all brushed down and washed off," she said haughtily, and tossed her reins to the young wrangler standing nearby. Putting a smile on her face, she turned and waved at Jake as he walked toward her.

"Jake, you're back from Dallas. I was beginning to wonder how long you planned to be gone."

"I didn't go to Dallas," he said, his tone flat and hard.

"Oh, well, I'm glad you're back anyway. It's just not the same around here without you." She brushed off the front of her jeans and pushed several strands of long, inky-black hair from around her face.

The truck and trailer pulled in near Jake's pickup.

"Well, let's go up to the house and—." Barbara's smile faded as she saw Clanci and Harlen climb down from the truck.

Jake turned.

Clanci didn't want to distrust Jake—in fact her heart was telling her she was being a fool—but her grandfather wasn't convinced of Jake's innocence, and she couldn't deny there was still a shadow of suspicion eating at her too.

Barbara was Jake's sister, and Blue had been at Walker Acres. Could she really have pulled that off without Jake's knowing?

"This is Harlen and Clanci James," Jake said, watching her. "From the Lazy J next door."

Clanci felt like crawling into a hole. It was obvious from the look she'd seen in his eyes when they'd met hers that he knew she was there because she didn't totally believe he was innocent. That tore at her almost as much as the disappointment she'd seen in her grandfather's eyes when he'd figured out that she had fallen in love with Jake.

She stiffened against the feelings. She had to know the truth.

"Clanci. What a delightfully different name," Barbara said as she moved past them. "Well, our neighbors are always welcome at Walker Acres. Please, come into the house."

"Rather walk into a damned cageful of hungry coyotes," Harlen grumbled.

Horrified, Clanci nudged his arm, then grabbed it, forcing him to accompany her. "Grandpa, please." She kept her eyes averted from Jake's as they followed Barbara into the main house, settling in a large living room kept private from the ranch guests.

In spite of the emotions churning within her like a whirlwind, Clanci found herself momentarily appreciating the room's decor, from the colorful Indian print on the furniture to the authentic Navajo blanket on one wall and the collection of Kachina dolls lining the mantel.

She also took note of how Barbara moved as she walked across the room, all grace and beauty. If the woman had had a couple more inches of height, she could easily have had a career as a top fashion model instead of a public-relations executive.

"I'll have Maria bring in some iced tea," Barbara said, and pressed the intercom that sat on the end table.

"Make it coffee," Jake said.

She looked at him queerly, her long dark lashes narrowing over pale blue eyes, then she ordered the coffee and sat back in her chair. "Is something wrong, Jake? You seem rather grumpy." Her gaze slid over him. "And, now that I notice, you look a bit rumpled." She glanced at Clanci and Harlen. "Not exactly kosher for company."

Jake propped a booted foot onto the coffee table, laid his arm over it, and glared down at her. "Yeah, Barb, you could say something's wrong."

Her gaze darted from Jake, to Clanci, to Harlen, and then back to her brother. "Well, just tell me what I can do to help out. But—"

"You stole my damned horse, that's what's wrong," Harlen bellowed, bounding to his feet. "You and that damned brother there, who's trying to act so innocent-like."

Clanci watched Jake's reaction. He didn't move, he didn't look at her, and she didn't know what to make of that. Wouldn't an innocent man jump up and deny her grandfather's accusation?

Barbara glared at Harlen. "We didn't steal anything of yours, Mr. James. We have our own horses, which are of top blood, so why would we want anything you have?" she said haughtily, the implication that Midnight Blue was inferior to her horses hanging in the air. She turned her gaze toward Jake and frowned. "Please take your foot off the table, Jake."

He didn't move. If he hadn't known about the PR firm, about how her boss had accused her of ruthlessly setting out to sabotage another account exec's reputation and underhandedly stealing his largest account, he might never have suspected, or believed, she could do this. But he did know, and because of that, he knew she was all too capable of sabotaging the Jameses, and even stealing their horse, if it meant getting what she wanted.

"You've been trying to run the Jameses off their property, Barb."

Her brows soared and Clanci noticed her hand move to absently finger one of the buttons on her blouse. "What? Run the—" She shook her head, glancing at Clanci and Harlen, and then back at Jake. "Oh, this is ridiculous. How can you even accuse me of such a thing. I'm your sister."

"You never sent a salesman over to their place with a couple of offers, supposedly from me, to buy them out?"

"Of course not."

" 'Cause they was from *you!*" Harlen said, staring at Jake.

Jake ignored both Harlen and Clanci and continued to stare at his sister. "You didn't cut any of their fences?"

Barbara shot out of her seat. "I don't know what you're talking about, Jake. How can you even ask me something like that?"

A muscle clenched in his jaw. "You didn't set fire to a stack of hay in their east pasture, Barbara? Or have one of your flunkies do it?"

"No. That's absurd." She turned away and walked toward the French doors that looked out onto a terraced patio. "I don't even believe you're asking me these things."

Clanci didn't know how she knew it, but she knew that Jake hadn't known what his sister was up to. He was as innocent as he'd claimed. She felt such a rush of relief and joy, she could barely restrain herself from jumping off her chair and throwing herself into his arms.

"You didn't destroy one of their gates?" Jake said.

Barbara whirled around to glare at him. "No."

" 'Cause probably *you* did that one," Harlen grumbled, his gaze pinned on Jake.

Clanci felt her heart sink.

"And you didn't steal their stallion, Midnight Blue?" Jake said, his attention never wavering from Barbara.

She again began to finger the button. "Of course not. I didn't even know they had a stallion. And why would I want to steal it?" She stalked back to stand near him. "What is this all about?" She turned a nasty glare on Clanci and Harlen. "Did you cook up this phony accusation so you could sue us? Is that it?"

Just then Henry pranced in through the open French doors.

"Oh! Get that dirty bird out of the house," Barbara said, stomping a foot on the soft white carpet.

The phone on the end table rang.

Startled, Barbara jerked around, then grabbed for the handset.

Jake slid his foot from the table and, turning, walked into the hall.

"Hello?" Barbara said, glancing toward the doorway through which Jake had disappeared. "No, I'm sorry, I can't talk now, I . . ."

Jake appeared back in the doorway, a cordless phone held to his ear. His eyes met Barbara's and dared her to hang up. He walked into the room and, setting the phone down on her desk, pressed the

hands-free button and placed the phone on the coffee table.

"Barbara, honey, dang it, are you there? I'm telling you, we got a problem."

Clanci recognized Sheriff Rick Murdock's voice
instantly.

"That's that mealymouthed—"

Jake held up his hand to shush Harlen.

"Barbara, I—"

"Rick, I'm really busy," Barbara said. "We'll
have to talk another time."

"Busy, huh? Well, who isn't, sweetheart? But
like I said, we got a—"

Clanci felt a start of surprise at the endearment.
Rick and Barbara?

Barbara looked around the room nervously,
averting her eyes from her brother's. "Rick," she
said.

"—problem," he continued, ignoring her efforts
to shut him up. "The stock truck arrived at the
slaughterhouse, Barb, but Midnight Blue wasn't on
it. You don't think that driver pulled a funny one on
us and sold him on the road somewhere, do you? I
mean, I don't see any other way. . . ."

Clanci's jaw dropped open as shock swept
through her.

Jake leaned forward toward the phone, his eyes
never leaving Barbara. "Sheriff, this is Jake Walker."

There was the sound of a sharp intake of breath,
then silence.

"Sheriff, you all right?" Jake said, as if he were the epitome of concern.

"Barbara?" Rick said, sounding suddenly panic-stricken. "Barb, honey, are you there? What's going on? What's your broth—"

"I think my sister is the least of your worries right now, Sheriff," Jake said. "Actually, I have a suggestion for you." He sent Barbara a withering stare. "You see, things are going to be changing a bit. Barbara's going to be moving out of state within the next few days and—"

Barbara bristled. "I am not," she said, her face a mask of outrage.

The dark brow over Jake's right eye cocked skyward as cold anger emanated from his still features. His sister's momentary outrage seemed to disappear. He turned his attention back to the phone, and Rick Murdock. "Now, as I was saying, Sheriff, I suggest that you start looking for another job. Preferably out of state, and most likely not in law enforcement."

"Listen here, you," Rick Murdock blustered, "nobody tells me what to do. I'm the sheriff and I—"

"You *were* the sheriff," Jake said. "Now you're nothing more than a thief."

He glanced at Clanci and she started. *You should have believed me.* She saw the words in his eyes, felt them in her heart.

"Find yourself another job, Sheriff," Jake said. With that, he quietly hung up the phone.

"Jake," Barbara said, putting down her own phone and moving toward him, "you have to understand." Arrogance rather than entreaty laced her tone. "We need unrestricted access to the river, and they wouldn't sell. It's the only way we can expand our operations and compete against the other large dude ranches in the country. We need more activities. We need to have free access to the river. We're already making a profit, but we could be making more."

"You're leaving, Barbara," Jake said. A thread of steely menace edged his voice.

Barbara stiffened, and stared at him in defiance. "I own half this ranch, Jake."

"Let me know where you settle, Barb. I'll send you a check."

"I'm not selling out."

A dark smile pulled at Jake's lips. "Then you'll go to jail."

Shock registered on Barbara's graceful features, and she stepped back from him. "I'm your sister. You wouldn't do that to me."

Jake shook his head. "Thankfully, I don't have to make that decision." He glanced over his shoulder toward Clanci and Harlen, his meaning clear. He might not press charges against his sister, but Clanci and Harlen would.

Barbara paled as the reality of the situation became all too clear.

"You've got twenty-four hours, Barb," Jake said with a contempt that forbade further argument.

She flashed him a look of disdain. "You'll be sorry, Jake," she said stiffly. "You can't make a go of this place without me."

He shrugged. "Maybe not your way."

Her eyes blazed with the same amber fire Clanci had seen in Jake's eyes when she'd had him hog-tied to her bed. Spinning on her heel, Barbara stalked from the room.

The pent-up breath Clanci had been unaware she'd been holding suddenly burst from her lungs in a long sigh of relief.

Jake turned at the faint sound. "You still weren't sure I was on your side, were you?" he said.

The warmth that had been in his eyes earlier when he'd held her, kissed her, wasn't there. Fear, like nothing she'd ever felt before, touched Clanci's heart.

"No, I . . . I mean . . ."

The sound of Barbara's boots on the ceramic tile of the foyer echoed through the room.

Jake stiffened.

Barbara looked at Jake, then at Clanci. "I finally figured it out," she said. "It took me a few minutes, because I was too busy being shocked by your accusations, but it's her, isn't it?" An ugly laugh ripped from her lips. "I should have known you weren't thinking with your brains, brother dear." She shook her head and rolled her eyes in disdain. "Is this like last time, Jake? Like with Katherine? Did you fall instantly head over heels?"

"That's enough, Barbara."

Her eyes flashed defiance. "I helped you through that one, Jake, remember? I was there for you when Katherine walked out on you."

Clanci's mouth dropped open.

"Barbara," Jake said with a snarl.

"When she decided that you weren't quite good enough for her, I was the one there to pick up the pieces for you, Jake." Barbara laughed haughtily. "You were pathetic. But who'll be here to help you pick up the pieces when Little Miss Cowgirl walks out on you, Jake?"

"My life isn't your concern anymore," he said stiffly, humiliation and anger bristling through him.

Barbara glared up at him. "You're right, it isn't," she said. "And my life isn't your concern." Before anyone knew what she was about to do, her open palm slammed against his face. The crack of flesh slapping against flesh seemed to echo through the room.

Jake's head jerked to the side and he took a surprised step backward.

King Henry suddenly squawked and charged Barbara.

"Get that monster away from me!" she screamed, spinning around and running for the door.

Henry took off in hot pursuit.

Clanci stared, dumbfounded.

"That's the way, bird," Harlen hooted. "Give her a good peck for me too."

The door slammed behind Barbara, and the

house suddenly became quiet again, except for Henry's soft and satisfied cluckings. Harlen, still chuckling softly, turned to a bar that was set in a corner of the room. "Think I'll have me a little snort," he said to himself. "Kinda celebrate."

Jake turned to Clanci. "Satisfied?"

She started at the coldness of the word, and the hard look in his eyes.

"Jake . . ."

"I'm sorry for the trouble my sister caused you," he said. "Send me a bill for the damages to the fences, hay, and whatever." Turning on his heel, he walked from the room without another word.

Clanci looked after him, every emotion in her body ripping to shreds. It was over between them. In a matter of days she'd fallen in love with a man she thought she thoroughly disliked, and now he'd walked out of her life because she hadn't trusted him enough to believe him.

She turned to her grandfather. "C'mon, Gramps. It's time to go home."

"But I'm . . ." He looked at the drink he'd just poured.

Clanci walked out. "I'm leaving, Gramps," she threw over her shoulder. "Catch up to me when you want."

Jake paced the intricately landscaped courtyard outside of the kitchen where Barbara had fed her guests their gourmet "Dude Ranch Brunch."

How could he have been so stupid? For months she had done nothing but bristle at him, reject every invitation he'd offered, and act as if he were nothing better than roadkill. Then she'd drugged and kidnapped him, and he'd fallen head over heels for her.

He was crazy. That was the only answer. And he'd get over it.

An hour later he knew he was lying to himself. By the time he got over Clanci James, he'd probably be dead and buried, his body turned to dust and his presence on earth not even a memory to anyone.

Clanci topped the hill that looked down on the James ranch house and her own cottage. "Finally," she said softly.

"Well, we wouldn't be out here walking if you wasn't so stubborn," Harlen grumbled. "Least you coulda let me do was have that wrangler give us a ride back."

"No."

"Women," Harlen said. "Never can make up their minds about anything."

"You don't like him, so what are you grumbling about?" Clanci snapped.

Harlen eyed her long and hard. "Whether I like him or not don't matter," he said. "It's what you're feeling, here." He thumped on his chest over his heart.

Clanci started down the hill. "Well, it doesn't matter. It's over."

The words had no sooner left her mouth than the roar of an engine cut through the silence and Jake's pickup came into view on the drive below them.

Clanci's heart nearly stopped.

Jake climbed from the truck and bounded up to the cottage door. He banged a fist on it, then walked inside. A second later he reemerged and looked around.

Henry pranced around the yard.

Jake cursed under his breath. The woman was driving him nuts. One minute she acted as if she believed in him, loved him, and the next she was looking at him as if she suspected he might be out to steal her blind. He yelled at Henry, then stalked around to the driver's side of his truck. It was probably a mistake coming there anyway. If she loved him, she would have believed in him. He was reaching for the door handle when he spotted Harlen and Blue on the hill nearby.

Clanci was halfway down and walking toward him.

He waited until she paused a few feet away from him before he spoke. "When we made love," he said, calling on every ounce of courage he had, "did it mean anything to you?"

She hadn't expected that. Shock ripped through her like a jolt of lightning. His words swirled through her head, tears filled her eyes, and she lost the capacity to swallow. The air became suffocatingly hot. Her knees felt weak, her heart threatened both to stop beating and beat itself into an explosion. She licked at lips suddenly as dry as the desert, and rubbed palms together that seemed to drip with moisture.

"Clanci?"

She looked up at him with eyes so full of tears that he was little more than a blur before her. "Yes," she said softly. "It meant more than . . ." She couldn't go on. How could she tell him it had meant the world to her? That he'd stolen her heart and until that very moment she hadn't even realized how completely?

"Then why didn't you believe in me? Why didn't you trust me?" His voice was hard, his eyes dark.

"Because I told her if she did, she wasn't my family no more," Harlen said, walking up behind Clanci.

Jake never took his eyes off of her. "But that wasn't all of it, was it, Clanci?"

She shook her head, ashamed. "No," she said softly. "I was afraid. I'd been so wrong about Alex. I was afraid I was wrong about you too."

"Do you still feel that way?"

She looked up at him through her tears. "No," she said softly.

His tight expression relaxed into a smile that was so magnetic, Clanci found herself wanting to reach up and caress his lips with the tips of her fingers.

Emotion stuck like a knot in his throat, and he struggled to force it back down to his heart, where it belonged. "I love you, Clanci." He'd never thought he would say those words to a woman again after Katherine, but the moment Clanci had turned away from him back at his ranch and started talking about going home, he'd known he didn't want her to leave him—ever. "But if there's any hope for us, any tomorrows, you have to trust me. Completely. Can you do that, Clanci? Can you love me enough to trust me completely?"

"Say yes, girl," Harlen whispered behind Clanci.

She suddenly felt as if she was going to burst from the happiness rushing through her. "Oh, Jake."

Before he knew what she was about to do, Clanci threw herself against him, her arms wrapping about his shoulders. "I love you too," she said, standing on tiptoe and raining kisses all over his face. "I trust you, I love you, I do, I do."

He exhaled a sigh of relief, mingled with the first real sense of contentment he'd felt in a very long time. A deep laugh rumbled from his throat as he held her tightly against him. "Well then, since we have that settled, will you marry me?"

A sudden eruption of squawks, howls, and hisses broke out around them.

Glancing over her shoulder, Clanci laughed as she saw King Henry charge through a corral in hot pursuit of Buster and Fluffles. She turned back to Jake. "Yes," she said, laughing. "Yes."

EPILOGUE

A year later Clanci brought home Queenie, a beautiful snow-white hen, and King Henry instantly fell in love.

Midnight Blue's first colt took top honors in one of the biggest horse shows of the season, making Blue one of the most sought-after studs in the country.

Walker Acres and the James Ranch merged to become the biggest working cattle ranch and horse-breeding operation in the state.

Harlen decided to retire and let Jake do all the work, and started courting the Widow Higgins, who ran the bakery in town.

And Clanci told Jake he was going to be a daddy.

THE EDITOR'S CORNER

It is with much regret and a heartfelt sadness that I offer you a glimpse of next month's LOVESWEPTs, the last treats we will be able to present to you for the holidays. The December books will be the final romances published in the LOVESWEPT line. Savor these special holiday gifts from four of your favorite authors. Like every book we've published, they are truly keepers.

In the final chapter of the Mac's Angels series, Sandra Chastain brings you what you've been waiting for. LOVESWEPT #914, **THE LAST DANCE**, is Mac's very own love story. What would it take to get Mac to leave his secret mountain compound, Shangri-la, where he runs Angels Central? A chance to meet Sterling Lindsey turns out to be too much of a temptation for him to resist. Working for Mac's friend, Sterling has had enough contact with the mysterious head of the network of angels to know there's something special about him, something that draws her to him. On the way to their meeting she finds herself in mortal danger, and her faith in Mac is put to the test. Forced into hiding, they confront emotions they'd never dared confess. In this story of risk and romance, Sandra sends a lonely hero into the greatest battle of his life: to save the woman who'd kept his hope alive. Don't miss the outcome when the man who's played angel for everyone else finds his own bit of heaven.

Mary Kay McComas knows that simple pleasures are the best life has to offer, and she reinforces that idea in **BY THE BOOK**, LOVESWEPT #915. Ellen Webster is a self-described nice person. It's when she decides she's too nice for her own good that things begin to go awry. With assistance from a little self-help book, she sets out to reach for the stars, to go for the gusto in life . . . and Jonah Blake represents gusto with a capital *G*. The man everyone in town has been talking about has been watching Ellen with avid interest. While Jonah is minding the town's camera store for his ailing father, he can't keep his attention away from the beautiful redhead in the bank across the street. When Ellen and Jonah finally meet, it seems as if they're playing right into destiny's hands. But Ellen begins to worry that he's falling for the wrong woman—the New Ellen. In this wonderfully touching romance, Mary Kay teaches us once again that it isn't always necessary to reach for the stars when everything you could ever want is right here on earth.

No author captures the flavor of the South better than Charlotte Hughes, and **THE LAST SOUTHERN BELLE**, LOVESWEPT #916, is quintessential Charlotte. Heroine Annie Bridges had all the advantages growing up, but her father controlled her every move. When he handpicks a husband for her, Annie decides to show her rebellious side . . . and she chooses a fine time to do it—on her wedding day! She steals her father's limo and races off in her gown, not realizing until she's fifty miles out of town that she hasn't a dime to her name. Enter the hero, Sam Ballard, an attorney/business owner who is talked into giving Annie a job as a waitress at his diner. Annie is the worst waitress he's ever employed— and the most attractive. But after working closely with her, Sam discovers she has hidden talents for accounting and sales . . . and a few of a more intimate nature. Annie can't envision life with a confirmed bachelor such as Sam, but life without him is a bleaker prospect. As they begin to fall for each other, the past catches up with Annie, and she faces the toughest choice of all. Charlotte is sure to make you laugh through your tears with this, her final LOVESWEPT.

It is fitting and appropriate that we end LOVE-SWEPT with a romance by Fayrene Preston. Fayrene was among the six authors whose books were featured in our first month of publication, way back in May 1983. She has touched the hearts and minds of so many thankful readers that there was no question who would write the very last LOVESWEPT. And what a book it is! Ending her Damaron Mark series, Fayrene treats you to **THE PRIZE**, LOVESWEPT #917. With his cousins Sin and Lion happily paired off, Nathan is the last eligible Damaron. In Paris on business, he goes for a walk and is startled beyond belief when a beautiful woman runs up to him, throws her arms around him, and says, "Would you mind kissing me as if you're madly in love with me and are never going to let me go?" Of course, he complies with her request, but when she runs off with only a thank-you, Nathan is mystified . . . and intrigued. Before he can search for her, she shows up again, this time with an apology and an explanation. When Danielle Savourat discovers the man she kissed as part of a game is a Damaron, she realizes she must clear the air. What she doesn't realize is that Nathan has no intention of letting her get away this time. Fayrene sets a steamy course for these lovers as they learn what can happen with just one kiss.

With thanks and gratitude for your loyalty to LOVESWEPT,
All best wishes,

Susann Brailey

Susann Brailey

Senior Editor